Praise for the Food Lovers' Village Mysteries

"A pleasing read with a thoughtful heroine, a plethora of red herrings, and some foodie tips."

—Kirkus Reviews

"A lighthearted and amusing story with the added bonus of several yummy recipes."

—Mystery Scene

"*Treble at the Jam Fest* has all the necessary elements to satisfy cozy mystery lovers: likeable, believable characters, a fast-moving plot, and a logical ending. Great fun!"

—Suspense Magazine

"A delicious mystery as richly constructed as the layers of a buttery pastry. Wine, enchiladas, and song make for a gourmet treat in the coziest town in Montana!"

—Krista Davis, *New York Times* bestselling author of the Domestic Diva Mysteries

"Leslie is a fellow foodie who loves a good mystery and it shows in this delightful tale!"

—Cleo Coyle, *New York Times* bestselling author of the Coffeehouse Mysteries

"Music, food, scenery and a cast of appealing characters weave together in perfect harmony in Leslie Budewitz's *Treble at the Jam Fest.*"

—Sheila Connolly, *New York Times* bestselling author of the Orchard Mysteries and the County Cork Mysteries

"Small-town charm and big-time chills. Jewel Bay, Montana, is a food lover's paradise."

—Laura Childs, *New York Times* bestselling author

Books by Leslie Budewitz

Food Lovers' Village Mysteries

Death al Dente
Crime Rib
Butter Off Dead
Treble at the Jam Fest
As the Christmas Cookie Crumbles
Carried to the Grave and Other Stories

Spice Shop Mysteries

Assault and Pepper
Guilty as Cinnamon
Killing Thyme
Chai Another Day
The Solace of Bay Leaves
Peppermint Barked
Between a Wok and a Dead Place

Destination Murders Short Story Series (Contributor)

"The Picture of Guilt: A Food Lovers' Village Short Story"
(in *Murder in the Mountains*)
"Seafood Rub: A Spice Shop Short Story" (in *Murder at Sea*)

More Books by Leslie Budewitz

Nonfiction and Cookbooks

*Books, Crooks and Counselors: How to Write Accurately About
Criminal Law and Courtroom Procedure*

Contributor

*The Cozy Cookbook: More than 100 Recipes
from Today's Bestselling Mystery Authors
The Mystery Writers of America Cookbook
Writes of Passage: Adventures on the Writer's Journey
How to Write a Mystery: A Handbook by Mystery Writers of America
Promophobia: Taking the Mystery Out of Promoting Crime Fiction*

Writing as Alicia Beckman

*Bitterroot Lake
Blind Faith*

AN UNHOLY DEATH

A FOOD LOVERS' VILLAGE MYSTERY

LESLIE BUDEWITZ

An Unholy Death

This story originally appeared in the collection *Carried to the Grave and Other Stories* by Leslie Budewitz, copyright © 2021 by Leslie Ann Budewitz

Cover design and illustration by Dar Albert, Wicked Smart Designs

Beyond the Page Books
are published by
Beyond the Page Publishing
www.beyondthepagepub.com

ISBN: 978-1-960511-26-3

An Unholy Death

"Gentlemen. We'll have no such rough language in Murphy's Mercantile," Kate Murphy told the two loggers as she plucked their change from the drawer of the brass cash register and slid the coins across the glass-topped counter. "About the sheriff or anyone else. Besides, it's too pretty a day for talk about thieving."

Both men cackled, their bushy beards in need of a good trim, then dropped the coins into the pockets of their wool pants and gathered up their supplies.

"Thank you, Mrs.," the older one said. "We'll be well fed for another week in the woods. Maybe next time we come into town, we'll visit the barber." He gave her a broad, blue-eyed wink, as if he'd heard her thoughts about his beard.

"Off with you now," she said with a wave of her hand.

The men laughed. "She's a feisty one," the younger man told his companion, a beefy hand reaching for the brass thumb latch on the front door. "Paddy's got his hands full with her."

At that, Kate's embarrassment turned to anger. *Don't let it show,* she warned herself. *You know what they say about the Irish.* In less than two years, Murphy's Mercantile had gone from a supply tent to a whitewashed shack to this grand building made of locally fired clay bricks, with plank floors and wide display windows and milk glass lights hanging from the tin ceiling. Paddy had sunk everything he had into the business and she dare not do or say a thing that might jeopardize its future. *Their* future.

She'd been Paddy Murphy's wife for thirty-one days now, the last twenty-two here in Jewel Bay, Montana. The town wasn't anything like what she'd expected, nothing like their hometown in Wisconsin. Paddy had been honest in his letters over the six months before their marriage.

The older cousin of a schoolmate, he'd come from Ireland at twelve and worked hard to get a start in the new country. A boy she'd known but never given any serious thought, until he'd come back to Wisconsin for a visit last winter. They'd locked eyes in an understanding, though she'd just turned twenty-one, and when he left to return to Montana, they entrusted their courtship to the postal service and planned a late August wedding. Then what was already being called the Great Fire of 1910 swept through the region, endangering millions of acres and thousands of people. Thankfully it had spared this valley. After their wedding and two nights in a grand hotel in St. Paul and the long railroad trip west, here she was.

No, Jewel Bay was nothing like she'd expected. Both more, and less, and every day full of surprises.

"Don't you mind them," said a woman in a yellow dress, lace and a green ribbon trimming the stand-up collar. She wore no hat, the dark hair fashionably coiled on top of her head accentuating her height, and her warm smile eased Kate's tensions. Or maybe it was the hint of lavender that surrounded her. "The valley's full of men like that. More comfortable with squirrels and silence than a pretty young woman. I'm Laura Peterman. I think you've met my husband, James, at the bank."

Kate felt herself blushing again. Was that going to be the way of things, at least until she'd met all the customers and figured out where all the canned goods were shelved and who paid cash and who had credit? Surely the Petermans had credit. Paddy had shown her the books, but he'd gone out to make deliveries, leaving her here alone for the first time.

And she wasn't pretty, not by a long shot. Short and slight, with fair skin and hazel eyes, brown hair and a pointy chin. A heart-shaped face, if you wanted to put it kindly. She didn't look Irish at all. Paddy said maybe not, but she wore her heart on her sleeve as well as her face, and that made her the sweetest lass to him.

"Kate Flan—" she began, then corrected herself. "Kate Murphy. I'm not quite used to it yet."

Laura Peterman's lips curved, but there was less warmth in her expression this time. Had Kate offended her? She couldn't imagine how.

"We're so pleased with all that you and Paddy have planned for the Mercantile," Mrs. Peterman said. "Now that residents will be able to get everything they need right here on Front Street, more families will put down roots. Town will prosper."

"That's all Paddy," Kate replied. "I only take credit for marrying him. Shall we see if we can fill that order?" She gestured to the list in the woman's gloved hands.

When Paddy applied for a loan to build the Mercantile, in the heart of town, not everyone at Jewel Bay State Bank had been sure of him. The West, with its logging and mining camps that sprung up almost overnight and closed down almost as quickly, was full of get-rich-quick schemers. But James Peterman had grasped that Paddy was not just another itinerant Irishman out to make a fast buck. He had plans, for himself and for Jewel Bay. Peterman had been impressed by Paddy's sketches of the storefront and the columns of figures showing what he expected to sell in each of the first five years. When the loan came through, Paddy had written to her that he felt as tall and broad as the Douglas fir and Engelmann spruce that studded the nearby slopes, their future secure.

Now, the two women reviewed the list. Kate stacked cans of tomatoes and corn and peaches next to bags of flour and sugar on the long counter. Then she pointed to the list, in Laura Peterman's graceful cursive. "Those we'll have to order from Pondera," she said, the name of the bigger town thirty miles away still unfamiliar to her mouth. *Pahn-duh-RAY.*

"James is eager to teach me to drive his new Packard," Laura said, "but I'm content with driving the horse and buggy into town. I'm grateful to Miss Lang at the school for suggesting you take over my daughter's piano lessons. Elizabeth is improving already. You should come to the house and play for us sometime soon."

"I'd be delighted." Kate had seen the Petermans' large white house, as fine as any back in Baraboo, on the north shore of the lake. Elizabeth had talked about their grand piano.

"It's settled then," the other woman said, and laid a hand on her list. "I trust these other things can be delivered?"

"Yes, certainly." The man Paddy had hired to make deliveries had taken his last wages and left town, and they hadn't found a replacement yet. Paddy was doing his best, loading up the wagon and driving the mule himself, but the extra work was taking a toll.

"Very good. Put all that on our account, please, but I'll pay you now for some licorice for the children." Laura Peterman drew out a small coin purse.

"That is exquisite," Kate said. She'd always been drawn to shiny things. The monogram on the silver clasp read *LLC*, the initials of the first and maiden names smaller than the *L* in the middle. Monograms were a rite of passage for a newly married woman; she'd been stitching her own on linen towels in the evenings. "My older sister has one much like it, a gift from her mother-in-law when she married. How many children do you have?"

"Three." The other woman laid a coin on the counter and quickly thrust the coin purse into her kid leather purse. Kate lifted the lid of a large glass jar and pulled out three sticky black sticks.

"Do be careful on your way home," she said as she handed over the bag of licorice. "If there is a band of thieves, as those loggers said . . ."

"Hard to imagine in broad daylight, isn't it?" Laura Peterman said. "But yes, a woman must beware of danger, and keep herself safe."

May the Good Lord keep us all safe, Kate whispered as the front door closed.

"It's worrisome, Paddy, it is," Kate Murphy told her husband later after filling him in on the talk about the thieves. "And it wasn't just those two loggers, trying to rattle me. All afternoon, everyone who came in asked what I'd heard, whether they'd struck again, what Sheriff Gibson is doing to track them down. People are frightened."

"Daniel Gibson isn't the sheriff. He's a deputy, though an able man," Paddy Murphy replied. "I'm sorry you had to hear harsh talk on your first day tending our wee shop on your own."

It was not just "a wee shop." Kate was astonished that he had built this fine general store, as fine as any she had seen. Astonished that they owned it, determined to make it prosper.

"But you're not worried? We do keep some cash here, and heaven knows where you go making your deliveries."

"No, lass." He took her in his arms, there behind the counter, and she glanced around. They were alone. And they were married. After a long, sweet kiss, he released her, the look on his face echoing the joy in her heart.

She was married.

"Jewel Bay's a gem," Paddy said, "but there's grousers here just like back home. Men who'll grouse when it rains and complain when it stops. They're not wrong about the sheriff, but Daniel Gibson will find those lowlifes and give them what-for. Now, me, I've got to find a delivery man. I can't be headin' out all hours of the day with bags of nails and flour and whatnot."

"There must be someone. A man who can drive the motor car as well as the wagon." The Model T couldn't go everywhere; the roads were too rough, too rutted and steep. A man might own a horseless carriage, but if he owned a business, he still needed a horse. Or a mule.

"Aye, but who, lass? When you talk to the Good Lord, ask Him to give you a name."

"Think of your hand as a mama bird, your fingertips the beak dropping food into her chicks' open mouths," Kate told her pupil, making her own hand a bird pecking the air. "A firm but gentle touch."

Grace Haugen was a serious child of eleven, her blond hair caught above her ears by a pair of barrettes. She barely smiled as she bent her head over the keys. But she could play, even if she was more determined to do things right than to make a joyful noise.

The Flannery sisters had all taken piano lessons and learned to draw and paint, and after she'd finished school, Kate had given lessons in the parlor of the family home. So when Anne Lang, one of the Jewel Bay elementary school teachers, had asked her to take on a few pupils after school, she'd readily agreed. She and Paddy had no piano, not yet, though she hoped they would in a few years when they built a real house, maybe with an orchard and a view of the lake. But the battered oak upright in the smaller of the school's two makeshift classrooms was sturdy enough to withstand the pounding the children gave it, and it held a tune decently.

"LAH-dah-dah-da," she sang, leading the girl through the melody of the Bach bourrée. "Very good. That's very good. Now, let's add the bass line."

On they went, a phrase at a time.

"Good heavens," Kate said, glancing at the clock. "We've gone far too long. It will be getting dark. I'll walk with you and apologize to your father for keeping you."

They bundled into their coats—the October days were clear and sunny, but temperatures dropped with the setting sun. Grace retrieved her school bag and Kate followed her outside. The makeshift school in the church hall was cramped, but students and teachers were managing while plans were made for a new, dedicated school. No high school, though a handful of local students boarded in Pondera during the week to attend classes.

"Will your father let you practice on the church piano?" Kate asked.

"Sometimes," Grace said. "Though I think hearing me makes him sad. The first time he saw my mother, she was playing the piano in church. He always says that's what convinced him to serve God."

The girl's tone was serious, not quite grasping her father's joke. Kate had only met the Reverend Arval Haugen a time or two, but he struck her as kindly and gentle, if perhaps more attentive to his books and his flock than to his daughter. He might not notice that she was late, a thought that made Kate frown.

"His work makes him happy, Mrs. Murphy," the girl said.

"Of course it does," Kate said quickly, chiding herself for not keeping her feelings hidden. It was a fault, one her mother had cautioned her against many times.

"My mother played beautifully, almost as well as you, and she taught me as much as she could before she died. I wish . . ."

The words went unspoken, but Kate let her thoughts fill them in. *I wish she were here.*

They reached the minister's small frame house. It was dark, the chimney quiet. The gate in the white picket fence squeaked as Grace pushed it open, and Kate followed her into the yard.

"Where's Buster?" Grace asked.

The dog, Kate assumed. The reverend must be resting. She watched the windows, expecting a light to come on and the reverend to open the door and welcome them. Would he have supper ready for his daughter, or was cooking part of her chores? The parsonage had no garden that she could see, just a pair of young apple trees. Surely the churchwomen kept an eye on the absentminded widower and his daughter, dropping off spare eggs, beans, and potatoes.

But the house remained dark. Kate knocked and called out. Turned the handle and stepped inside, calling again. The house was neat and tidy and empty.

What should she do?

No point borrowing trouble. Most likely, he'd gone to visit a church member and lost track of time, as she and Grace had, though they'd been caught up in eighth notes, not tea and sympathy.

"Grace, does your father keep a horse and buggy?"

"He borrows one from Mr. Peterman or the sexton if he needs to go somewhere too far to walk or ride his bicycle."

It was a common sight, the man in black, a hat jammed on his head, riding a bicycle along Jewel Bay's dirt roads and up its hills, a speckled brown dog trotting beside him.

"Does he often go visiting this time of day?" *And leave you to fend for yourself.*

Grace nodded. "But he's always home in time for supper. Or nearly always."

Not the encouraging words Kate hoped for. "Well, shall we start supper?"

Inside, Kate turned on the lights. Thanks to Jewel Bay Power and Light and its capable manager, Ivan Gregory, most homes and businesses were electrified. Most had running water, too, though only a few had telephones, a service the power company had begun earlier in the year. After several tries, she got a flame going in the cookstove's firebox and put on a pot of water for the potatoes and carrots the girl was peeling. Though it was Wednesday, there was a good chunk of Sunday's roast in the icebox. She tucked the meat into a small roasting pan and added hot water. Before she left, she'd slip it in the warming oven.

Within minutes, the potatoes were boiling and the table was set for two. The kitchen was almost cozy.

"Well, then." Kate brushed one hand against the other. "Your father will come home to a nice hot supper. You can start your schoolwork while you're waiting." She hated to leave the girl alone, but it wouldn't be long, and she wasn't a small child. Grace would be fine.

"Thank you, Mrs. Murphy."

"Remember." Kate pinched her fingers together as she had during their lesson. "Like a bird," and the girl smiled.

Outside, dusk had deepened and it would be full dark by the time Kate got home.

But something tugged at her. She pulled her coat tight and retraced her steps to the church, a simple frame building so different from the brick-and-stone St. Joseph's in Baraboo with its spire and bell tower, the church where she had been baptized and married. As she approached, a dog came running toward her and stopped at her feet. His paws were muddy, and he smelled like pine pitch.

"You must be Buster. Where have you been?"

In the shrubbery beside the main doors, a bicycle leaned against the white clapboards. Just as she'd thought. Clearly, Grace had not noticed it. Kate herself had only seen it out of the corner of her eye, the sight not entirely registering.

She opened one heavy door. The air was still, though it bore a hint of the wax used to polish the pews and altar table. Not a large space, no bigger than the Mercantile. And empty.

To the left of the raised altar were two closed doors. One, she suspected, led outside, the other to the reverend's study. She'd give him a piece of her mind. What was he thinking, sitting here with his books and prayers while his daughter sat home alone, pretending not to worry?

She started across the nave, her hand already raised to knock. Glanced to her right, for no reason that she could explain then or afterwards.

Behind the altar table, on the raised wooden platform, lay a man in black. Crumpled—knees bent, one arm outstretched, hand open. His eyes were open, too. They'd once been blue, she could see, but the color had begun to leave them, as it did in the first few hours after death.

That, and the bloody gash on his forehead, a good three or four inches long, told Kate Murphy beyond any doubt that the Reverend Arval Haugen was, in fact, dead.

Ivan Gregory motioned Kate back, but she followed him anyway. She'd already seen the body; seeing it again was not going to make her nightmares worse.

The power company manager crouched and placed two fingers on the side of the reverend's neck. He was one of those men who, like Paddy, seemed to know exactly what to do in a difficult situation, and as soon as he answered her knock on his door, listened to her story, and stepped into action, her worry had eased. Not that everything would be all right; it would not. A man was dead, and a motherless girl now fatherless, too.

Gregory raised his eyes to hers, his expression confirming what she already knew.

"Would you offer a prayer, Mrs. Murphy, while we wait for Deputy Gibson?"

After finding Reverend Haugen, she'd gone outside, not wanting to check for a telephone in his office, and had seen the light on up the road in Gregory's two-story yellow house. She'd stood inside the front door while he telephoned the deputy. When Kate fretted about leaving Grace home alone, he'd instructed his nephew, a slender boy of about twelve, to fetch Miss Lang, the teacher, and escort her to the parsonage to sit with Grace. The boy asked if he should come to the church afterwards, a mix of horror and excitement in his eyes, but the uncle had said no, he should stay with the women, and it was clear from the way the boy straightened his shoulders and nodded solemnly that he took his duty seriously.

What sort of prayer could an Irish Catholic and a Scot, as Gregory's name suggested he was, say together over the body of a dead Norwegian? No matter. They were all Americans. Montanans. God's children.

She cleared her throat and Gregory bowed his head, hands clasped in front of his chest. "Father in Heaven, we ask you to receive the spirit of Arval Haugen into your hands. To forgive his sins and accept him into the company of the angels." She paused briefly, wondering if Mr. Gregory or Reverend Haugen believed in angels. "You who listen to the cries of the injured and bereaved, who cares for the orphans . . ." Her words faltered, as she thought of Grace.

The church door opened. A tall man in a brown wool suit removed his hat and entered.

"Ma'am," Daniel Gibson said, a hint of the South in his voice. Her mouth opened and closed without a word. Then he acknowledged the power company manager with a quick nod. "Ivan."

She had met Daniel Gibson once, when he'd come into the Mercantile to see Paddy. With the county seat so far away, the residents of Jewel Bay were fortunate, and grateful, to have a resident deputy. Who the two men were who came in behind Deputy Gibson, she couldn't say. Locals he'd rounded up to assist if needed? She had no idea what might be needed. One man stepped into the small office and a moment later, the electric sconces mounted on the walls began to glow.

Oh, how she wished Paddy were here. He'd be locking up the Mercantile and heading home, expecting to find her working in the kitchen. He'd worry at her absence, with the band of thieves on the loose. But he knew she was giving lessons; if it got too late, he'd come to the school to fetch her. Dismay over worrying her husband vied with her concern for Grace, and she shuddered.

"Good of you to come so quickly," Ivan Gregory said, and Kate was struck by the stiff formality of his tone. What could be the reason? Surely she was imagining things, in the terrible moment.

"Doc is on his way," the deputy replied.

Gregory gestured to the body. Gibson stepped onto the altar and crouched to check for a pulse, then leaned closer to inspect the wound on the dead man's forehead. Raised the man's outstretched hand, turned the wrist gently, then laid it down again. Stood and let his gaze move slowly around the room. It stopped at the altar table, continued its circuit, and returned to the table.

"Where are the candlesticks?"

They all looked around, as though the missing objects were simply waiting to be noticed.

"Tall. Silver. Matching pair." Gibson held one hand about ten inches above the other. "A gift from a parishioner. Most valuable thing in the place, I suspect."

"The thieves?" Kate asked, surprised to hear her voice shake. "Could—could they have done this?"

"You never know what a greedy man will do, Mrs. Murphy, I'm sorry to say," though Gibson didn't sound sorry. "You shouldn't be here. One of my men will take you home. We'll get a search party going."

"I'll wait for the doctor," Ivan Gregory said, as much to her as to Daniel Gibson, who did not reply, already discussing plans with his men.

Kate found herself reluctant to leave. She hadn't known Arval Haugen well—she didn't know anyone in town well aside from Paddy. But she'd liked him and was genuinely fond of his daughter. This wasn't her church—there was no Catholic church in Jewel Bay—but their God was her God, and as Deputy Gibson's man took her elbow and led her out, she sent a quick prayer upward, asking God to send His comfort and strength to all those in need.

And His mercy, and justice.

"I can't take her home with me," Anne Lang whispered as the two women huddled in the kitchen of the parsonage, the cookstove radiating a warmth Kate's every bone craved. "Not with Frank . . ."

The teacher's younger brother, who lived with her. There was something wrong with him. Kate didn't know what.

The deputy's man had wanted to take Kate straight home, but she'd insisted on coming here. The wagon had barely stopped when the dog bounded past and threw one paw against the front door. Grace had opened it, seen him, and raised her face to Kate. "Where's Papa? What's happened?"

Now Kate glanced at the teacher in her navy skirt and white blouse, blond hair braided on top of her head, her back stiff and her eyes wary. It was Kate who'd found the man, and she who had to break the news.

"Let's sit," Kate said, gesturing to the kitchen table and taking the seat across from the girl. "I'm so sorry, Grace. We don't know exactly what happened. He—he may have tried to stop some thieves and been attacked. He's—"

"He's dead, isn't he?"

Kate nodded, not trusting her voice. It had never failed her the way it had twice in half an hour. But then, she had never before found a man dead or had to tell his daughter.

Grace's eyes filled, but she didn't cry.

"Mr. Gregory is with him," Kate continued. "In the church. Deputy Gibson is starting a search party. You'll come home with me for the night. There's a man waiting outside with a wagon."

Anne Lang touched the girl's shoulder. "Go pack your nightgown and clothes for tomorrow."

Wordlessly, the girl rose and left the room. Anne sank into the empty chair. "How could such a terrible thing happen? Such a good man, and that poor child."

"I lost track of time on our lesson—she's making such progress. The school was dark when we left. So was the church."

"I walked right by it, but I didn't notice a thing."

"Did you see the reverend's bicycle?" Kate asked. "Against the wall by the front door." Of no interest to the thieves.

"No. Best to keep her home tomorrow. Give her a day to let the news sink in."

What was she going to do with a grieving eleven-year-old? "Has she no family in the area?"

"No." Anne got to her feet. "I'll be off now. My brother will be wanting supper, if he's home, though I can't stomach the idea. Let me know if she needs anything. I'll talk with the other teachers and students tomorrow."

The two women stood, silent. Kate grasped Anne's hands and they locked eyes. Not quite friends, but not quite strangers, drawn together by tragedy. And by the needs of a young girl.

Anne left and Kate made her way to the girl's bedroom. From the doorway, she watched Grace tuck a small pile of clothing into her carryall. Then she took a framed photograph from the top of the oak dresser and slipped it into her bag.

Her mother? A family portrait?

"Ready, then?" Kate asked gently, only to see a tear sliding down Grace's cheek.

And she folded the sobbing girl into her arms.

Kate's spirits lifted at the sight of lights in the window of their little log house, a beacon in the gloom. The wagon slowed, the front door opened, and Paddy emerged, summoned by the sounds of wheels and hooves. He was in his shirtsleeves, his suspenders dark against the white shirt, his sandy hair catching the light behind him. Kate didn't wait to be helped but grabbed her skirt and jumped.

"Paddy, oh Paddy!" she cried as she ran to him.

"Slow down, lass. What's a matter with yeh?" He caught her by the arms and she searched his face. He didn't know. He looked past her to the man and child in the wagon. "And who's this?"

"Oh, Paddy," she said again, then explained about finding Reverend Haugen dead in his church. Paddy listened, his fair skin paling beneath the freckles, concern in his wide blue eyes. By the time Kate finished her story, their escort had helped Grace down and brought her to them, the child clutching her small bag, the dog beside her. Kate lifted a hand to touch her shoulder, then pulled it back.

"It's gotta be them thieves," the man said. "Daniel Gibson's getting up a search party."

"I'll get my coat and my rifle," Paddy said. "If you'll wait on me a minute or two. Obliged to you for bringing my wife home. And the girl."

Kate led Grace inside, Paddy following.

"Paddy, no," Kate said. "You're not going with them."

"I am, lass. They'll need all the men they can get. The Model T would be faster, but I can't be sure of the roads where we'll be going." He tugged on his coat, then spoke in a low tone. "I'm taking the rifle, but you've got the shotgun. And the dog."

She'd almost forgotten about the dog.

"Yeh'll be all right, you and the girl," he said.

Would she? Would they? They had no telephone at home. The closest neighbor was well out of shouting distance. If the thieves were bold enough to strike in town, in daylight, would they target the Murphys, assuming a shopkeeper with a fine new brick building was prosperous, never mind that it was built on borrowed money? Never mind that their cash was locked in the Mercantile's safe, and that they owned little else of value?

She almost laughed. Any thief with his wits about him would see this place, barely more than a cabin, and ride on by.

Daylight, she thought, her mind spinning backwards. Would thieves strike in daylight, so close to the school and homes where they might be seen?

"We'll be back before yeh know it," Paddy said. Then he kissed her on the cheek, picked up his rifle, and was gone.

Kate stared at the door. Reached out and locked it.

"Well, then." She blew out a big breath. The girl hadn't eaten; she'd been waiting for her father. Kate hadn't eaten in hours. Wasn't sure she could keep anything down. Not after seeing the reverend's vacant eyes, the bloody gash. "You'll have to sleep on the sofa. It's a bit scratchy, but we'll find you a spare quilt. And light the fire, if we need to."

"Please, Mrs. Murphy," Grace said. "May I have a bowl to give Buster some water?"

"Oh, good heavens. Yes." Kate led the way to the kitchen, where she filled a good-sized enamelware bowl—small as the place was, at least Paddy had been able to bring running water inside, though he'd never gotten around to bringing the outhouse in. She set the bowl on the floor, and the sound of the dog's tongue lapping up the water seemed to fill the room.

A few minutes later, after she'd shown the girl where to put her things and the privy out back, they dished up the supper they'd brought with them, not wanting it to go to waste. Grace cleaned her plate. Kate set hers on the floor for Buster, then put the kettle on. Cut two slices of apple cake.

What next? School work? Impossible. What else might a child do after school and chores and supper? When Kate had been Grace's age, she and her sisters had read, quietly or out loud. They'd sketched or sewn. Played the piano and sang. Here, most evenings, she and Paddy talked. He'd tell her about the customers. Who was setting up a homestead or building a barn. Who came in hoping to sell extra produce or wool, or hoping he'd take a lamb in trade. The sewing machine he'd ordered for the doctor's wife, and where on earth would he find a new delivery man. Her husband could talk the ears off a hollow tree, but she loved every minute, every tidbit, as he told her about Jewel Bay and the logging camps and the steamships that plied Eagle Lake, the farmers nearby, the Indians who crossed the valley.

But Paddy wasn't here. She had to figure this one out on her own.

She poured boiling water into the porcelain teapot and set a glass of milk on the table for Grace. They sat, with their cake.

"I haven't gotten used to the quiet yet," Kate said. "Back home, in Baraboo, I lived with my parents and the sister just above me. My younger sister is attending art school in Chicago, if you can believe that. She's only eighteen, but so talented."

Grace lifted her fork to her mouth, her gaze fixed on Kate. Her eyes were sad, but not afraid, and clearly interested, so Kate went on.

"My oldest sister, Alice, is married and lives a few blocks from our parents. Her husband is on the railroad, as our father was before he retired. She's got two little ones and they drop by almost every day. So there is always something going on."

"Where's Baraboo?"

"In Wisconsin. Not far from Madison, the capital."

"My grandmother lives in Chicago."

"Oh." The tea had steeped by now so Kate poured herself a cup, steam from the dark liquid carrying the rich, floral aroma of the Darjeeling her mother had sent with her. Paddy sold a rough, inexpensive brew. He wasn't convinced yet that more subtle varieties would sell, but she was sure that as the town grew and more ladies settled in the area, they would need to stock a few finer things. "Your father's mother or your mother's? We must write and let her know what's happened. Or telephone her in the morning, from the Mercantile."

"My mother's mother," Grace said softly. "But she won't care."

Kate was taken aback. Her maternal grandmother, small and Irish and always in black after being widowed at thirty-seven, had lived with them as long as Kate could remember, until her death a few years ago. Her father's parents had farmed outside of town and she had seen them every Sunday of her life until they too had died, months apart.

"Do you have other relatives? In Montana, by chance?" Though Anne Lang had thought not.

"Not that I know of."

"We'll write your grandmother tomorrow," Kate said. "I'm sure she'll be deeply saddened."

Grace's jaw tightened and she lowered her eyes. "No. She won't. She warned my mother against marrying my father. She said he was a dreamer and an idealist who could never support a wife and children. My mother died when I was eight, and my grandmother told my father it was his fault, that he had no one but himself to blame and we were not welcome in her home again. That's when he decided to move west, and the bishop sent us here."

Kate was shocked. How could the woman speak so cruelly? Out of grief and anger, yes, but even so . . . Perhaps she'd softened. But Kate could not say that. She could not raise false hope.

She leaned forward, a hand on the table. "You are very young to be alone in the world. I believe Deputy Gibson and his men will find your father's killers and bring them to justice, but that will take time. Meanwhile, you'll be safe and cared for."

Was that enough? It was all she could say, all she could promise, right now.

Grace set her hands in her lap and lowered her chin. It quivered, and she caught her lower lip with her teeth. Buster leaned against her leg, and she rubbed his boxy head and scratched behind one floppy brown ear.

Then the dog laid down, the girl picked up her fork and took a bite, and Kate let out her breath.

She had more questions, but they could wait. She'd as much as promised to keep the girl for now. What Paddy would think, she could scarcely imagine.

After they'd finished their cake, Kate washed up the dishes. "What did you and your father do in the evenings?"

"He read, or worked on his sermons. Sometimes I read to him."

"Oh, what an excellent idea. Would you like to read to me, while I work on my sewing?"

Grace's eyes brightened. "Miss Lang lent me a book of poems. I could read from that."

Kate switched on the electric lamp in the front room—she couldn't pretend the cramped, low-ceilinged room with its log walls was grand enough to call a parlor—and Grace rummaged in her bag for the book. Kate picked up her sewing basket and sat on the sofa beside the girl. Drew out the troublesome tea towel, an elaborate M traced lightly on the creamy white fabric. So graceful, so perfect before she pierced it with her needle. Needlework had never been her talent. Her sister Alice could make the needle sing, but in Kate's hands—well, it was as if the fabric turned grubby and the stitches crooked almost before they were done.

"My mother could sew anything. She made all my clothes as well as her own. Papa likes to say—" Grace interrupted herself, swallowed hard, then spoke again. "Papa liked to say there wasn't anything she couldn't make, or make prettier with a bit of lace."

Kate returned the towel to the basket. "Tell me about her."

And Grace talked. She talked about her mother's soft gentle hands and the tenement in Chicago where they lived while her father served the poor. About her father's determination to make a home for the two of them, serving God and the people of Montana. She talked about school and books she'd read and how hard the piano was and how much she loved it. She talked about the dog. She talked until she fell asleep. Kate slipped off the girl's shoes and slid her legs onto the sofa, turned out the light, and sat in the kitchen with another cup of tea and the dog and the eddy of her own thoughts swirling like the rushing waters of the Baraboo River until Paddy came home.

The dog lay at Paddy's stocking feet. Paddy had kept watch when he let the dog out to do his business, making sure he didn't try to find his way down the hill to the parsonage. But the dog seemed to know this was where he needed to stay, close to Grace.

"Hide nor hair," Paddy repeated, cake finished, a fresh cup of tea in front of him. They were going to need a third kitchen chair. Maybe they could bring one from the parsonage. Although it belonged to the church, not to Reverend Haugen. Did the chairs belong to the church, too? Grace had said the bishop sent them here. He would have to be notified and a new minister chosen—she didn't know how Protestant churches worked. Grace had also mentioned the sexton. Would he notify the bishop?

"We couldna find a trail from the church, so Gibson led a group down the banks of the Jewel and along the bay. Sent another over to Eagle River." The town sat above the bay that joined the Jewel River to the big Eagle Lake, not far from the outlet of the larger Eagle River. "I joined up with Ivan Gregory and Thaddeus London and another Scot, and we scoured the lakeshore. Came across a camp of Piegan, smoking their fish this side of the big river."

"The Piegan. One of the Blackfeet tribes?" She'd seen Indian families a few times since her arrival, first from the train, then when they'd taken the Model T and camped in the brand-new Glacier National Park, christened this past May. Some people feared the Indians, called them savages or worse, but she saw no reason for that kind of talk or distrust. A band of Menominee had lived near her grandparents' farm, and her grandfather had often traded with them and let them hunt in the woods down by the creek.

"That's right. London wanted to roust 'em, but they were no more than a couple of families doing no harm." Paddy cradled the thick white mug. "This does a body good, Kate, your fine tea and your cake. The air's beginning to take on a chill, and tramping around like that, never sure what we'd find . . ."

He pressed his lips together and shook his head, and she was grateful she'd been able to give him some comfort, slim as it might be.

"Will you join the search again tomorrow? In the daylight?" she asked. *Daylight.* The word kept pestering her.

"Not me. The shop won't run itself. I'm good for identifying who's been in and out, who's new in town, but I'm not so good at reading signs and trails of men on the run."

She didn't believe that for a minute. Far as she could see, Paddy Murphy could do anything he put his mind to.

"They're long gone by now, I expect," he continued. "Spending the night in a camp deep in the woods, or in an old homesteader's shack."

She thought of the two loggers who'd been in the Mercantile today. Not that she suspected either of them. But there were plenty of men on their own in these parts, working for themselves, living alone or in pairs, some quite rough. They came into Jewel Bay or Somers, the mill town across the lake, to sell their labor and pick up supplies, and otherwise went unaccounted for, except by a sharp-eyed shopkeeper. Not like life back in Baraboo.

"Paddy, about Grace."

She felt his blue eyes on her.

"We have to keep her, Paddy, until it can be decided what's to be done. She has no family to speak of. Her father's people are all gone. Her mother died three years ago, and the only relative she knows of is her grandmother, who blamed Reverend Haugen for her daughter's death and wanted nothing to do with him or Grace. I'll write to her, of course, if we can find an address, but it could be weeks before we hear. I know quarters are tight, and it's another mouth to feed, but we've got to do right by her. I can't let the sheriff send her to some orphanage in Helena or God knows where. She's just a girl, Paddy, a smart, sweet girl alone in the world."

Paddy set his mug on the table, stood, and wrapped his arms around her. "Darling Kate. Your heart is bigger than you are. We'll keep her as long as need be. And don't worry about feeding her. You married a grocer."

"And the dog?" Buster had raised his head at the disturbance, then lowered it again.

"And the dog."

Kate felt her body soften, her heart open, tears flow as she embraced this man. *Her husband.* Who grew up with so little and was so determined to make a life for her, for them, to make their shop the beating heart of this rough diamond of a town.

Kate sat up. What was that sound? Was someone lurking outside?

She ran a hand over her forehead, brushing back the fine hair that had escaped her braid. Yesterday's events came back to her, a rush of tangled memories. The thieves. Reverend Haugen, dead on the altar of his church.

The girl. *Grace.*

The dog.

That's what she was hearing. Kate slipped out of bed, careful not to disturb Paddy, and pulled on her dressing gown. She found their guests in the kitchen. At some point during the night, Grace had wakened, no doubt surprised to find herself asleep on the Murphys' sofa, fully dressed except for her shoes. She'd changed into her nightgown, visible under her coat, her feet bare inside her shoes, as she attempted to work the pump over the iron sink to refill Buster's water after his predawn trip outside.

"Let me help you," Kate said. "It sticks sometimes." It was a long reach for a short woman like her, and naturally, this was the moment that the handle decided to get good and stuck. Finally, using all four hands, the two managed to raise the handle and set the water flowing. Grace filled Buster's bowl and Kate filled the kettle, and between them, they managed to get the handle down, then traded looks, stifling giggles.

That's where they were when Paddy walked into the kitchen, in pants and undershirt, his mustache damp.

"And what female shenanigans do we have going on here?"

Grace's brow wrinkled and she bit her lip, but Kate could see Paddy's eyes were twinkling.

"Sit, you two," she said. "Out of my way while I get breakfast on."

At the word "sit," Buster sat. So did Grace, still wrapped in her coat, in Paddy's chair. Paddy disappeared and Kate began cracking eggs and frying ham. She enjoyed cooking, though the kitchen was small and cramped, and the cookstove temperamental. Memories of mornings in her mother's kitchen came unbidden, the chaos of four girls, her big-bellied father grinning as they teased and poked each other. What did Grace remember of mornings with her mother? What would she remember of her father, and of this painful time?

Paddy returned with a wooden crate, which he placed at the side of the table with a gesture that made clear that would be his seat, and Kate gave him a grateful look. At her direction, he chopped leftover roast and potato for the dog. The collies at her grandparents' farm had eaten table scraps and chewed on bones not meant for the soup pot. They'd have plenty for the sturdy brown critter. Then Paddy poured Grace a glass of milk—they didn't keep a cow but bartered with a neighbor, and the pitcher was running low, so she'd have to take care of that.

The water boiled.

"When I was a lad," Paddy said to Grace as he made the coffee, "my ma and pa eked three, sometimes four days of brew out of one pot of grounds. That's how poor we were. By the fourth day, the stuff was so weak you could see right through it."

Kate glanced over her shoulder and saw Grace smile.

"And I told myself," he went on, his brogue growing thicker as the tale grew taller, "that when I was a man, I'd make my coffee so strong you could walk across it."

Grace's smile widened.

Kate set plates of fried eggs and ham on the table and took her seat. Paddy perched on the crate and reached for her hand, then Grace's. The girl hesitated, then took it.

"Bless us, Lord God," Paddy said, "and this food we are about to eat, thy gift. Thank you, Lord, for keeping young Grace safe from the evil that took her father from her. From us. He was a good man, and we know you are welcoming him to your flock. We ask you to guide Deputy Gibson and his men as they continue their search, so we may have justice in this world as well as the next. Amen."

"Amen," Kate repeated, and heard Grace echo the word in a small voice.

Breakfast over, Paddy finished dressing and left for the Mercantile. Kate let Grace wash and dress in their bedroom, no bigger than it needed to be but more private than the front room, then took her own turn, putting on a dark burgundy skirt Alice had made for her and a white blouse. When she came out, Grace was sitting in the kitchen, Buster at her side, her book open on the table. She'd washed the plates and forks and left them to dry on a towel on top of the cabinet beside the sink.

"I didn't know where you keep the dishes."

"That's just fine, Grace." Kate poured herself the last of the coffee and added a splash of milk. It wasn't as strong as Paddy liked to claim, but close.

But the moment she sat across from the girl, a wave of despair struck her. As the third of four, Kate had not spent her own childhood looking after younger ones. She'd watched Alice's children many times, but they were small. Not eleven like Grace, her mind and body changing by the day, orphaned in shocking circumstances. Kate and Paddy wanted children, naturally, but she expected—her mother and Alice had assured her of this—that she'd learn by doing when they came along.

So that's what she'd have to do now.

First task, baking. Three pies—one for Miss Lang, and at Grace's suggestion, another for Mr. Gregory and his nephew. The boy lived with his uncle during the week so he could attend school—he was a year ahead of Grace—and went home to his parents' farm on weekends. Grace chatted easily as they peeled and sliced the apples, but after Kate placed the last top crust and slid the pies into the oven, she saw that the girl's eyes were moist, her skin pale.

"Do you want to tell me about your father?" she asked. "He seemed like a good man."

"Oh, he was, Mrs. Murphy. He was the best father in the world," Grace blurted. "I don't care what my horrid old grandmother says about him. He loved my mother and he loved me, and everything he did, he did for us. And for God, but for us first. Is that a terrible thing to say?"

"No, not at all." She led the girl to the table, where she sprinkled two bowls of sliced apples with sugar and poured in the last of the milk. "I think taking care of the people closest to us is the best way to serve God. We can't help others until we do that, can we?"

Arval Haugen, she learned, had been orphaned as a small boy and farmed out to distant relatives, good godly people by his daughter's account, who had never met the couple, now long gone, except through her father's stories. He'd been cared for, loved even. It was a common enough story, but her heart ached to think of the cycle repeating itself with Grace.

"What happened to the farm?" she asked. Perhaps it had remained in the family, a family who would welcome his only child.

"It was lost in the Panic."

The Panic of 1893, which had changed so much for so many. Kate had been small herself then, but she'd heard talk.

"And he met your mother in church, playing the piano?"

"In Chicago, during his theology training. His classmate was engaged to her best friend and invited him to go along to her church for services. They stood up for each other at their weddings."

Might this couple take her, if the grandmother didn't come through?

"They're missionaries in Africa," Grace continued. "They write to us about the people they meet and the strange plants and animals. I got to tell their stories to the other kids when we studied Africa in geography class."

So they could not take the girl. But she should write to them as well.

They finished their fruit, and Kate asked the question she'd been dreading. Better that she know the answer before Deputy Gibson questioned the girl.

"Grace, did anyone dislike your father? Except for your grandmother. What is her name?"

"Agnete Swensen. My mother was Freya, and I'm Freya Grace."

"A lovely name. Can you think of anyone who might have wanted to harm him? Anyone he argued with, or who threatened him?"

"He didn't argue with anyone, Mrs. Murphy." Grace clasped her hands in front of her. "No one."

But clearly, someone had taken their rage out on the reverend. It was good that the girl had been protected from that evil. But if she didn't know, who did? Kate did not believe that any thieves smart enough to know the value of two silver candlesticks would carry out their bold burglary when they were likely to be seen. When the presence of the dog and bicycle suggested that someone might be in the church, even if they didn't know it was the reverend himself.

"Did he seem worried?"

Not that Grace knew. There had been no unusual visitors. Mr. Peterman had come by to discuss church finances, and Miss Lang had dropped in to ask if there were any funds to pay her brother for doing odd jobs. Grace thought the answer was no; most church work was done by volunteers. If any volunteers had seen anything suspicious, they would tell the deputy. Whom Kate prayed would find the killer soon.

While the pies cooled, they tidied up. Then they packed Paddy's lunch and the pie and headed for the school. It was impossible not to pass by the church. Grace walked very close to Kate, who took her hand and squeezed it.

They found Anne Lang seated at the desk in her empty classroom, her pupils playing in the yard between school and church. Smells of chalk and woodsmoke mingled in the air. At the sight of them, she rose.

"Mrs. Murphy. Grace. I didn't expect to see you today."

"We brought you a pie," Grace said and held out the basket with the warm pie, wrapped in a white tea towel. A plain towel. Kate dare not share her ragged embroidery with this accomplished woman, beside whom she felt young and awkward.

"Thank you." The teacher took the basket. "Frank will be particularly pleased. I manage a decent Sunday roast, but pie is beyond my meager kitchen skills."

Kate had seen Frank Lang in the post office across the street from the Mercantile. One shoulder was lower than the other and he dragged one foot behind him as he walked. She guessed him a few years younger than Anne, but it was hard to tell.

"We were also hoping to pick up some schoolwork for Grace," Kate said. "So she doesn't fall behind."

"Little chance of that. She's one of my best pupils. But I'd be happy to find a book or two. Grace, why don't you fetch your slate, so you can practice your sums? You can take a fresh piece of chalk from the cupboard." The girl obeyed and the two women moved toward a bookcase on the far wall.

"How is she doing?"

"Well, I think. She's talked about him, and her mother, and cried a little, which I think is good. Less than I would have, but she seems a stoic child. If that's the right word."

Anne Lang nodded. "It's good that she's with you. You're kind, but no-nonsense."

Kate wasn't entirely sure that was a compliment.

"Not that I would expect any nonsense from Grace. She's eleven," the teacher continued. "Almost a young lady. I am not of the opinion that children should be protected from unpleasant truths that affect them. They simply need to be spoken with in a way they can understand. Grace is intelligent and imaginative. Her mind will fill in what she doesn't know, and what she imagines may well be worse than the truth."

Kate shuddered. Anne Lang had not seen the body. She had.

She took the books. "Grace told me that you came to see her father a few days ago. Possibly to ask about employment for your brother—she wasn't sure."

Anne's jaw tightened and her shoulders stiffened.

"Did he seem worried to you?" Kate continued. "Did he mention any—oh, disagreements?"

"You're asking if I know who might have wanted to kill him."

Kate felt herself flush.

"And no." The teacher's tone softened. "As I told Daniel Gibson, I don't know who could possibly have done such a wretched thing."

At the sound of footsteps, they turned to see Grace, holding her slate against her chest, her gaze darting from one woman to the other.

"Mrs. Murphy, I'll take your students for the rest of the week," Anne Lang said, then smiled at Grace. "We'll give your star pupil a few days off."

Kate handed Grace the books and the girl sat at the nearest desk, turning pages.

"I'd like to keep her out of school another day, if you think that's advisable. She can make a fresh start on Monday. You're sure she has no family other than the grandmother?"

"I'm sure. Have you spoken with her about the funeral?"

Kate had barely thought about that. Anne touched her arm. "Don't give it another thought. The sexton and church members will take care of everything."

But as Kate gathered up her young charge and started off for the Mercantile, she thought of little else.

Woman and girl made their way to the town's growing business district. At the north end stood the Jewel Bay Inn, built earlier in the year, a two-story white frame structure with a high false front and a porch that spanned the width of the hotel.

On the west side of Front Street stood the Jewel Bay State Bank, as impressive as any back home. A man on his way out tipped his hat and offered his condolences, as did others they met. Word of the reverend's death had spread like the fires of last August.

An empty wagon parked in front of the Mercantile reminded Kate that Paddy might need to make deliveries this afternoon, requiring her to keep shop for a few hours. Even when he hired a delivery man, he was counting on her to work by his side. The prospect was both exciting and frightening.

"There's my bride," Paddy cried when she pushed open one of the double doors. "There's my Mrs. Murphy."

A cheer went up from the men clustered in front of the hardware display and Kate knew her skin was betraying her.

Then Paddy caught sight of the girl. "Hush now," he said. "It's

Reverend Arval's girl she's got with her and we want to show the man our respect."

The hubbub stilled. One of the men stepped forward and stood in front of Grace. "Aye, lass," he said in a thick Scottish brogue. "Your father was a good man, doing good work. Never a harsh word, never a quarrel."

There was a general murmur of agreement. But had that been true, Kate asked herself, one hand on Grace's thin back. Had the man been killed for a reason, a quarrel, none of them suspected?

The place was busy. Kate set the basket with Paddy's lunch on the steps to the tiny office under the eaves. Showed Grace where they hung their coats, then plucked her apron off another hook.

"What a beautiful day," she said to the girl. "The season will be changing soon. You might sit on the bench out back and read one of the books Miss Lang gave you. Keep the mule company."

"Can't I help you? And Mr. Murphy?"

"I suppose you could."

For the next half hour, Kate took orders and packed up groceries, while Paddy tended to men at the hardware counter. Grace stayed close to Kate, fetching items she pointed out, loading bags and baskets.

"I'll be off making deliveries, lass," Paddy said. The shop was empty but for the three of them. He pulled his apron over his head and handed it to Grace. "Way too big for yeh, child, but yeh might as well put it on."

She did, looking pleased, though Kate had to knot the neck strap to hold the apron up and wrap the ties twice around her middle.

"Don't forget your lunch," Kate said.

"My stomach would never let me." Paddy kissed her cheek. "I'll be back before dusk. If there's anything you can't find, or orders you aren't sure about, we'll figure it out later."

He grabbed his lunch basket off the steps. Then the back door closed and they were alone. *I'm only ten years older than she is*, Kate thought. Ten short years.

Though the customers when she arrived had all been men, the female side of town streamed through in the afternoon. Women from the church, or mothers of Grace's classmates, who offered her a quiet word or a quick embrace. Kate blinked back tears at their thoughtfulness, a reflection of their esteem for the reverend and their understanding of the girl's loss.

"So good of you to take her in," a woman said while Grace's attention was elsewhere. "It must have been dreadful, finding him the way you did."

Dreadful, sadly, did not begin to describe it. Twice during the night, Kate had cried out at the memory and sat up, pressing the heels of her hands into her eyes while Paddy wrapped his arms around her.

What else could she have done? It might have been her Christian duty, as another woman had said, before recalling that Kate was Irish and a Catholic, but Kate hadn't acted out of duty. She hadn't intended to take the girl at all until it became clear that Anne Lang could not keep her, but in that moment, her mind had been made up.

"It's no trouble," she said. "Grace is a lovely child. Your total is one dollar and seventeen cents."

She gathered up the bits of advice the women gave her, and gratefully accepted their offerings of bread and a few extra eggs. Yes, the Murphys sold groceries, among other things, but Kate understood that bringing food to the house of the bereaved—for that's what they had become, with the addition of Grace—was a way to extend condolences. A way that people instinctively took care of those around them in times of sorrow. From her customers, she learned that the reverend had not just prayed with those in need, but organized members of his flock to provide food and firewood for the family of an injured man, given an impoverished widow train fare to return to her parents' home, and performed other good deeds both expected and unexpected of a man of the cloth. She heard no hint of animosity in the talk, but fear edged in when two women mentioned that their husbands had joined another search party today. Until the thieves were captured and brought to justice, children would walk home from school in groups, or their mothers would come to walk with them. These women would keep their families home after dark, and bar their doors.

She learned, too, that the sexton and other male volunteers had scrubbed the blood off the wood floor. A group of women were busily airing out the church and cleaning it from top to bottom, washing the windows and floors and polishing the pews with bees' wax to make them gleam. Cleaning, too, was an instinctive response to loss, especially one so harsh and abrupt.

But like her, they had not touched the reverend's office. They'd leave that to the minister from Pondera, when he came on Sunday to preside over the funeral and burial.

That seemed too soon, but it wasn't. Yesterday, the day of the murder, had been Wednesday. What made it seem rushed, Kate realized, was that the death had been so unexpected. She had not yet had time to notify Agnete Swensen, though if Grace were right, that would make no difference. And even if she had, where else would Arval Haugen be buried but here in Jewel Bay, the site of his church as well as his death? He had no family to welcome his body home. His wife had been buried with her people, and it seemed unlikely that Mrs. Swensen would spare room in the plot for her murdered son-in-law. The farm was gone, the town a part of his past. He had no home ground but this. How strange it would be for Grace, if she did return to Chicago, to leave her father behind.

But despite the women's kindness, Kate fretted. She had known life here would be nothing like life in Baraboo, in the cocoon of the Flannery family home dominated by her mother's strong presence and her father's steady hand. She had known this was the frontier at the edge of the untamed wilderness. Front Street lacked a boardwalk, although some businesses, like the inn and the bank and the Mercantile, had built their own. Volunteers had regraded the street this past summer on "Good Roads Day." But despite the residents' efforts and ambitions, Jewel Bay was raw and unfinished.

Could she be the helpmate Paddy needed, a trusted figure behind the counter that townspeople would rely on, as they did him?

Never mind all that. Today, she had to figure out where the extra canned peaches were, how to adjust the scale, how to deal with the leering faces of the lumberjacks who came in for beans and potatoes and salt pork and the prying eyes of the society women, such as they were, wondering what sort of wife and woman this slip of a girl so new to this great big roaring state of Montana might turn out to be.

She straightened her shoulders and got to work.

Midafternoon, Grace was deep in conversation with a stout woman of about sixty, no taller than she. A member of the church, Kate guessed from the woman's comforting tone and gestures. Grace looked more at ease than Kate had ever seen her, except at the piano.

The door opened and Laura Peterman entered. She glanced around the shop, spotting Grace, and her lips curved.

"I see you've put the child to work."

Kate cursed her fair skin, flushing again. Would she ever learn to control it?

"I mean no judgment," the elegant woman said as she pulled off her gloves. Today's dress was a pale peach, almost too pale for the season, but not quite. Again, a hint of lavender surrounded her. "Only that it's good to keep children busy. Not that anything will keep her mind off what happened. Or yours."

So she knew that Kate had found the body.

"What can I get for you today?" she asked, eager to steer the conversation away from the tragedy and her handling of it.

"Not a thing. My husband is in important meetings all day, so I decided to drive the buggy in and gather the children from school. And I wanted to let you know Elizabeth will not be able to attend her piano lesson today. I'll pay you—"

"No, no," Kate said. "Miss Lang is giving the lessons today, and I am certain she won't mind."

"Good. And how is Grace? That's the doctor's mother-in-law

speaking with her, by the way. A very good soul."

"Ah, thank you. As for Grace, she's a brave child. Sweet, and very helpful. She has no family other than a distant grandmother. I'll write to her, but I am not sure what the future holds."

"As none of us is," came the reply, and Kate wondered what unexpected hardships she'd endured. After a long moment, Laura Peterman spoke again. "I understand Deputy Gibson led a search party last night, but they didn't find the killer. Or killers. Have you heard any news today?"

"Only that another search is underway. Deputy Gibson seems competent. Paddy—Mr. Murphy—is certain he'll find the killer."

"Oh, I am sure he will," Laura Peterman replied. She was a genuinely pretty woman, with light brown hair and eyes of a golden brown. Kate's younger sister, so skilled in portraiture, would very much enjoy painting her. She was about to say so when Laura reached across the counter and touched Kate's arm with her ungloved hand. "Do let me know, Mrs. Murphy—Kate—what I can do to help you and Grace."

She called out a greeting to the doctor's mother-in-law, drew on her gloves, and left.

Paddy returned earlier than expected, freeing Kate and Grace to head home on foot to start supper. Grace was silent on the walk, and Kate wondered if she'd heard something she shouldn't have, in the conversations that had swirled around the shop that afternoon.

"We'll stop and pick up a few more things for you. I imagine your father kept an address book, so we can write to your grandmother." They were nearing the parsonage now.

"Buster!" Grace called and crouched to embrace the muddy dog racing to her.

"Good heavens. What is he doing here?" But it was obvious. The dog had seen no reason to stay at the Murphys' when Grace wasn't there. How much the dog understood about his master's death, Kate had no idea. But clearly, the dog knew Grace needed him. He licked her cheek, then laid his big head on her shoulder, one muddy paw on her skirt.

It will wash, Kate reminded herself. It was good for the girl to have a companion.

Kate had not taken a good look around the parsonage yesterday, and now she saw that it was sparsely furnished, the pieces mismatched, serviceable but well-worn. Donated, no doubt, by members of his congregation. Arval Haugen and his daughter had been in Jewel Bay nearly three years, but clearly, he had not been the sort of man who paid attention to homely details like whether the furniture matched or paintings hung on the walls. His mind had been on higher things. Her gaze fell on a small secretary, cherry with a glass-front upper cabinet, the mullions in an elegant diamond pattern.

"That was my mother's," Grace said. "It's the only piece of furniture we brought west."

Kate's breath caught in her throat. The upper shelf held hand-painted porcelain cups and saucers. Freya's work? She tilted her head to read the titles of the books on the lower shelves. Theology texts. She rummaged quickly through the notes and pamphlets tucked in the cubbyholes, but found no address book. Grace had no idea where he'd kept it, and Kate could see nowhere else to search in the tight quarters.

"Why don't you pack up your school clothes and a nice dress, dark if you have one, while I go see if I can find the address book in the church office?" A dark dress for the funeral, which they had not yet discussed. "And bring your piano music. We'll start our lessons again next week."

Grace agreed, and Kate went outside. The air was warm, though the birch and aspen leaves had changed color and begun to drop, and the afternoon would have been quite lovely had it not been for her difficult errand. As she neared the church, she wondered if she should have waited for Paddy to go with her.

Don't be a silly girl, she told herself. You're a grown woman. Now act like one. But it was nice to have the dog walking with her.

She decided to try the side door rather than go in the front, so she could duck into the office without passing by the altar. Despite the thorough scrubbing, she knew she'd never enter the church again without seeing the blood, the dead man, his beseeching eyes.

Without warning, the dog darted past her out of sight. "Buster. Come back here."

She followed him to the rear of the building, to a woodpile large enough to serve both church and school. The dog was digging furiously at the base of the pile, dirt flying from his paws.

"Buster, stop that! You'll bring the whole pile down." He'd already dislodged several smaller pieces. But that wasn't what momentarily stopped her heart.

In the opening he'd created, where a chunk of firewood should have been, was a gleaming silver candlestick.

After the discovery, Kate hesitated to dare enter the church. Did the school even have a telephone? The lines were new, the school location temporary. Besides, classes had ended, and with the Peterman girl not taking a lesson today, the building would be empty.

In the tidy homes up and down the street, children were doing chores and schoolwork. Fathers were returning from their work and mothers getting supper ready. She could not bring herself to disturb them.

"Kate Murphy, don't be foolish." She took a deep breath and straightened her filthy skirt, not bothering to brush it off. "Stay here, Buster."

First, she went back to the woodpile. Retrieved the candlestick and tucked it into her bag, then returned to the church. Marched in, pushed open the office door, and placed the call to Deputy Gibson.

"Fetch Ivan Gregory," the deputy told her. "Ask him to keep watch until I get there. Then take Grace home."

Why did he not simply call the man himself? Because he wanted her out of the way. Was that a harsh judgment? She'd had the impression the deputy didn't think a young woman, barely more than a girl even though she was married, had any business mucking about in murder. But she hadn't chosen to become involved. She'd found the body, and that gave her a responsibility.

Maybe she was misjudging him. Maybe he simply wanted to keep her safe.

Her, and Grace.

But she held her tongue. The muddy dog had waited for her outside. No one was in sight. She crossed the wide, dirt street and hurried to Gregory's house.

No lights in the windows and her knocking went unanswered. What should she do? Deputy Gibson had wanted the woodpile guarded. But she had left Grace alone.

At the sound of footsteps, Kate turned to see a man walking toward her. Though his dark cap was pulled low, she was sure she'd seen him before. In the shop, she supposed. A laborer. What was his name?

"Hello," she called, and the man stopped, raising his head in surprise.

"Why, if it isn't the new Mrs. Murphy," he exclaimed, sweeping off his cap and bowing in a theatrical gesture. It was quite silly, given his dirty work clothes and scuffed boots, and all that weighed on her mind, but even so, she found herself smiling, almost charmed. "Thaddeus London, at your service."

London. That was it. She'd heard the name from Paddy, though what he'd said about the man escaped her.

"I've come to see Mr. Gregory, but he doesn't appear to be at home."

"Noo. No, he's not. Fine place like this, but it belongs to the power company. I hear he's got his eye on building himself an orchard, on the edge of town," London said, jerking a thumb over his shoulder. "Might there be something I could help you with? A fine lady like you."

"I wanted—no. It's nothing that can't wait." Deputy Gibson had told her to summon Ivan Gregory. Yesterday in the church, she had detected a carefulness between the men, but no distrust. This London, though, seemed a different kettle of fish. Jewel Bay might be a young town, but it was like any other town that way, full of all kinds of men, and women, too, here for their own reasons. "But I thank you."

That should have been enough for the man, a dismissal, an indication to go his own way. But he did not. He kept his gaze on her a moment too long, and then another moment, and she had to remind herself not to show her discomfort. She had as much right to walk these streets as he did, as anyone did.

Then London flashed her a toothy grin. "Good day to you then, Kate Murphy."

She watched him saunter down the street and round the corner. "Go find Grace," she told the dog.

Buster cocked his head. "Go," she repeated. "Go find Grace." And off he trotted.

She followed at a distance, keeping an eye on London. As the man neared the church, he turned and waved, then kept on going down the hill. Aiming for one of the taverns, she guessed, or the boardinghouse. She watched until he was out of sight. She checked the woodpile, but it had not been disturbed any further. Then she scurried to the parsonage.

Grace was sitting on the front step, a book in her lap, a valise at her feet. A valise, and the dog.

Kate blinked back her tears, put on a smile, and marched toward them.

She might almost have been back in the house in Baraboo with her sisters, laughing, as she and Grace sponged the mud off their skirts, then started supper. Was it right to laugh, in a time of loss and fear? Or wrong not to enjoy the moment? What, Kate thought, did God want of us in such times?

At the sound of the automobile, she patted her hair. No need to pinch color into her cheeks, already pink from the heat. Paddy came in the kitchen door, as he usually did, and after hanging his coat on the hook, he took Kate in his arms and held her as tight as ever he had held her. He smelled of work, and leather, and the hay he'd fed the mule.

"Will you give us a minute, child?" he asked Grace.

The girl nodded and went into the front room, closing the door behind her.

"You're all right, then, lass?" He held Kate's shoulders and searched her face. "You and the girl?"

"We are. How did you hear? What did you hear?" She laid her hands on his and searched his face, her eyes hungry for news.

"All news passes through the doors of a general store, in any small town." He led her to the table and sat, then bent to unlace his boots. "Aye, and it's what I wanted my shop to be, but I do wish the news were better."

"Have they found anyone? Or anything?"

"The other candlestick? No. And what have you done with the one you found? What have you told the girl?"

"You tease me for carrying a big cloth bag instead of a lady's purse, but it came in handy. I didn't dare leave the candlestick behind. If the thief returned, no one would ever believe I'd actually found it." Kate sat across from her husband. "All I told Grace was that I hadn't been able to find her father's address book, that we'd have to search for it later. Truth is, I never got a chance to look. I went inside long enough to use the telephone and left. It was Buster who got the scent, good dog."

The dog lifted his head and sighed as Paddy rubbed one floppy ear.

This time, Grace insisted on sitting on the box as they ate, and Paddy said he'd stop by the parsonage and borrow a chair. "For now," he said lightly, acknowledging all they did not know. How long Grace would stay with them, where she would go when the time was right, and when another minister might be sent to Jewel Bay.

Kate had just put the wash water on to heat when a knock on the front door startled them. Paddy left the kitchen, still in his stocking feet, and a moment later, Kate heard Daniel Gibson's voice. She wiped her hands on her apron, then stood in the doorway, an arm around Grace's shoulders.

Deputy Gibson's dark eyes settled on her, his jaw tightening.

"If you've got any news, Daniel," Paddy said, "speak it plainly. No need to spare my wife. She found the reverend, you'll recall, and she found the candlestick today."

"Well, the dog found it," Kate said. Grace's thin body quivered and she tightened her grip. "And Grace is nearly twelve. She deserves to hear everything you know about her father's death."

But bad news—or good, for that matter—always goes better with a cup of something hot, so it was a few minutes before they sat, Grace on the sofa between Kate and Paddy, Daniel Gibson in the matching armchair, the bone china cup small and fragile in his hands. The candlestick Kate and Buster had rescued sat, partially wrapped in Kate's white handkerchief, on the mahogany coffee table her parents had given them as a wedding present.

"We tore that woodpile apart," Gibson said. "Searched every inch of church and school that we hadn't searched before. No sign of the mate, or anything else where it shouldn't have been. Tell me again, Mrs. Murphy, why you went looking for trouble in the woodpile."

"She's told you, Daniel," Paddy said. "It was the dog."

Gibson gestured with one hand. "And what on earth set the dog off? How did he know to dig there?"

His narrowed eyes made Kate wonder if he suspected she knew more than she should. That she'd been involved, somehow. Because it was strange that the same person—a woman, and a newcomer—had found both the body and the missing silver. People would stare. They'd talk. They liked her well enough, but they didn't know her yet, and they would talk. That's how small towns were.

"Buster sat at my father's feet every night," Grace said, speaking for the first time since Deputy Gibson's arrival. She glanced at Paddy. "Like he sits at yours, Mr. Murphy."

"Go on, lass," Paddy said.

Grace swallowed, then raised her eyes to Gibson's. "Buster went everywhere with my father. If he had a call to make, and it was close enough to walk, Buster walked with him. If he took his bicycle, when he went down to the lakeshore to visit the encampment or out to see Mrs. Peterman, Buster trotted along beside him. He waited by the front door to the church and barked to let Papa know someone was there to see him."

The Indian encampment. Kate had heard of it, but had not seen it. "I spoke with Mrs. Peterman this afternoon. She didn't mention a visit with the reverend. Did he go out there often?"

"No. Well, I don't know. Once, about two weeks ago? And Mr. Peterman came to see him at the parsonage."

Perhaps Laura Peterman was active in the churchwomen's guild. Churches depended on donors and volunteers, from those who paid for the candles and lights to those who scrubbed the floors and chopped the wood. And those who kept the records, a task for a banker like James Peterman.

"You're saying the dog might have seen what happened to your father," Deputy Gibson said gently.

"No one cares what a dog sees," Grace said, "because they can't talk. As long as he wasn't barking, the killer would have ignored him while he struck my father and left him there to die, then hid the candlestick in the woodpile. But Buster knew. And when Mrs. Murphy went to the side door, near the woodpile, he made sure she saw him digging and found the candlestick."

Kate squeezed the girl's hand, and Grace squeezed back.

Gibson sipped his coffee. Kate thought of the man she'd met in the street. No point mentioning him, though he had unsettled her.

"Deputy," she said, "no thief would leave behind the most valuable thing in that church. Nor would he have taken the time to hide it, once he'd killed a man."

"Why hide the one, though, and take the other?" Gibson said. "He has to have known it would be found. And one's not worth half what the pair would fetch."

True enough. Besides, if the thief tried to sell the single silver piece within a hundred miles, word would reach the sheriff.

"Might be it's hidden nearby, somewhere your men didn't search. Tossed down the hillside or into the water," Paddy suggested.

"Surely, though, the hiding means something." Kate leaned forward. "The candlestick wasn't simply dropped in the rush to get away. A killer bold enough to strike in broad daylight and then take the time to hide the candlestick in the woodpile wasn't a thief who got caught in the act and killed to cover his tracks."

The killer had known how to slip out one or two pieces of wood, hide the silver, then slip the wood back in. The killer knew how to stack wood. But then, almost every man did. Did the killer also know how much wood the church and school might use through the winter, and when the candlestick might be found?

"Mrs. Murphy, you've got a good head on your shoulders and I dare say there's a chance you're right. But the sheriff thinks the good reverend's mur—death the work of no-good drifters, and unless we find good reason to persuade him otherwise, that's the approach we'll be taking."

He was telling her to leave it be. To take care of Grace, and Paddy, and the things that a woman, a wife, should care about.

But it was clear to Kate that the discovery of the candlestick disproved the theory of killer thieves. It was equally clear that if Reverend Arval Haugen had been killed for some reason other than the missing silver, his killer might still be in Jewel Bay. And Grace could be in danger, too.

Deputy Gibson drained his coffee and set the cup on the table.

Stood, patted his pocket, and withdrew a slim black leather book. "Reverend Haugen's address book. Found it in his desk drawer, right where you'd expect."

Kate felt Grace's gaze, almost heard the girl realize Kate had lied to her about not finding it. A white lie, meant to hold off the moment when she had to tell the girl what she'd found. She vowed to tell no more such lies. They bought time, but caused pain in the process.

"Thank you," she said. "Grace, please fetch the deputy's hat and coat." While the girl did as she asked, Kate unwrapped the handkerchief around the base of the candlestick and pointed, wordlessly, at a dark red spot on the silver. Beside her, Paddy stifled a gasp and even the deputy grew more somber. She rewrapped the candlestick, then wrapped it carefully in a soft shawl. When he'd donned his coat and hat, the big man took the bundle from her as though it were a newborn baby, and headed out into the dark night.

The night was quiet, the only sounds an odd sigh or snort from the dog asleep on the kitchen floor. Dreaming of running beside his master, as the reverend pedaled out along the lakeshore to the Petermans' grand home?

The dog snorted and shuddered, and Kate wondered if he truly had seen the killer, had watched his master die.

With the door between the kitchen and front room closed, she could not even hear the faint ticking of the clock. Paddy was asleep in their bedroom, Grace on the sofa. Late as it was, though, Kate had no thoughts of sleep, certain that the moment she lay down, all that she'd seen in the past two days would play itself out against the darkness.

She cradled the cup of tea, its scent reminding her of home and the day she'd left to come west. She pictured her mother's fine dark eyes—Mrs. Flannery was a handsome woman—filling with love and tears of longing and excitement, all that had flooded through Kate herself. But of all the things she had imagined in her new life, she had not imagined finding a man murdered, or taking temporary custody of his daughter. She had not imagined listening to the deputy sit in her own home and tell her the sheriff believed the tragedy a theft gone wrong, though the evidence said otherwise.

"Lass, yeh may be right," Paddy had said to her after Gibson had gone. "But leave it be. Leave it to Daniel."

If there was a killer walking around Jewel Bay, were any of them safe? Could this be the haven Paddy and Ivan Gregory and James Peterman and so many others had worked so hard to create if a killer walked free because the sheriff had made up his mind?

She took a long sip, letting the toasty aroma and smooth, slightly sweet flavor soothe her. Then she set the cup in the saucer and opened her writing box. She threw two sheets of the creamy linen paper her sister Alice had given her as a wedding gift into the cookstove firebox before managing to complete a note she could bear to send to the formidable Agnete Swenson. Then she opened Reverend Arval Haugen's black book and copied out Mrs. Swenson's address, folded the letter, and slipped it inside the envelope. She'd forgotten to ask Grace the names of the missionary couple, and didn't want to flip through the book, searching for an address somewhere in Africa. Too much like prying.

So she poured another cup of tea and started a letter to Alice.

She was late. Since arriving in Jewel Bay, she'd written her mother every Sunday and her sister every Wednesday. But she could not have written last night, not with all that had happened. They shared her letters, although Kate trusted Alice to hold back any doubts or fears she expressed that might worry their mother. This letter was nothing but doubt and fear, and she wasn't sure she would send it. Alice didn't need to hear about the gash on Reverend Arval Haugen's forehead or the look in his sightless eyes.

Was it fanciful to even think she'd seen a look in them? A plea to protect his daughter and find his killer?

She'd always been too sensitive, Kate knew. Everyone had said so. Except Alice, who had held her and let her cry when they were at the farm and saw the colt break its leg. Alice had rushed her inside and held her hands over young Kate's ears but it hadn't been enough; she'd heard the gunshot anyway, heard the mare whinny long and loud. She could almost hear it now. Could almost hear Alice utter soothing sounds, hear her father tell her mother they couldn't baby her, she had to grow out of it. "Hush, Michael," her mother had replied. "Let her be. It's her big heart that makes her our Kate." If she tried to hold back her emotion, to say anything less than what she felt, Alice would know.

A tear splashed onto the paper and spattered the damp ink.

The door to the front room opened. Kate raised her head. Grace stood in the doorway, in her white nightgown, a wool shawl around her shoulders.

"Can't sleep?" Kate asked. "Sit. I'll warm some milk for you."

As she poured milk into a saucepan, the dog woke, stretched, and padded over to the table. Grace buried her face in his neck.

Kate set the mug of warm milk on the table. The girl took a long drink, then raised her swollen eyes to Kate's. "Thank you, Kate. For everything."

Kate nodded, not trusting herself to speak. Her tea would be cold now, too bitter for comfort, but she didn't want to busy herself heating more water, cleaning the pot, making a new cup. Sometimes it was better to stay put.

She touched the envelope on the table. "I've written to your grandmother. Would you like to add a note to her? I haven't sealed the envelope yet."

"What would I say?"

"What would you like her to know?"

Grace's fingers tightened on the mug, her knuckles almost as white as the milk itself. "That my father was a good man. That he loved my mother and me, and that he made a good life for us here in Jewel Bay." The shawl slipped off one shoulder and she tugged it into place.

Kate waited.

"That he never hated her," Grace continued, "even when she said hateful things about him. He believed everything he preached, about forgiving those who harm us. About praying for those who do wrong in the world."

Someone had hated Arval Haugen. Had done him wrong. Who? There could be no forgiveness until they knew who had killed him, could there?

How could she send this earnest, wounded little bird back to the woman who had sent her and her father away? Too lost, Kate presumed, in her own grief to stand the sight of the man who had loved her daughter.

"I've told her you're safe with us, for now," Kate said. "We can write her again in a day or two, when you're ready."

"Who else are you writing? I have no other family."

"My sister, Alice."

"Oh, the one with two children who lives near your parents in Bear— Bear what?"

"Baraboo. On the Baraboo River." The girl heard and saw everything, forgot nothing, just as in her piano lessons. They would have to be very careful. "Funny name, isn't it? I've heard half a dozen different theories about its origin. Most likely it came from a French fur trader who settled on the riverbank."

"What's it like, having three sisters?" Grace asked. "I wish I had a sister. Or even a brother. Miss Lang's brother lives with her."

You have me, Kate wanted to tell her, but held her tongue. Grace belonged with family. Perhaps there was an aunt or a cousin she didn't know about, someone who would open their arms and welcome her.

What if her ideas about her grandmother were wrong? Even a bright, perceptive child like Grace would not understand everything. Kate was counting on that, though the girl was so certain of the old lady's judgment that it would be difficult to persuade her otherwise, even if the woman wrote back immediately and extended every possible welcome. Even if she got on a train and came to fetch Grace herself.

And if the girl was right, and the grandmother did begrudge her existence but sent for her anyway? Should she be sent to a house where she would surely be alone, and lonely, even if warm and well-fed and educated? Sometimes children were better off in other situations, weren't they?

Don't be fanciful, Kate. You know nothing about raising children yet, let alone girls Grace's age. Although she had once been a girl Grace's age, interested in many of the same things. Not as drawn to books, but Grace had grown up alone with a bookish father.

"Come with me," Kate said, and led her back to the front room. On top of the side table sat several framed photographs, one of Kate and Paddy on their wedding day a month ago. Hard to believe so little time had passed—so much had happened. At the same time, her wedding day seemed like yesterday, so vivid. So happy. "My parents," she said, indicating a woman with strong features under a glorious sweep of dark hair and a man with a round head and a mustache, his railroad watch chain straining across the ample belly under his dark suit coat. "And this was taken last summer, just before Margaret left for art school, underneath the beech tree out back."

Grace held the photo of the four girls in both hands. Kate pointed at a woman who strongly resembled their mother. "That's Alice. Then me, and Margaret. And Mary, who's three years older than I. She's a teacher."

"Like Miss Lang."

"Teaching is an excellent occupation for a woman. You might consider it yourself."

Grace studied the photo for a long time, then returned it to the table and ducked behind the sofa. Opened her canvas bag and drew out a framed photo. Held it for Kate to see, but kept a firm grip. Kate did not try to take it from her hands.

"Oh, Grace. She was lovely." Freya Swensen Haugen had been a beauty, with wavy blond hair pulled into a loose chignon, a firm jaw and nose, and an enchanting smile. Kate glanced at Grace. Her face was still a child's, but if the maternal influence won, she too would catch eyes and hearts.

And in that moment, Kate understood how difficult the resemblance might be for Mrs. Swensen, and in her heart, she asked the good Lord to show them all the way.

The next two days, the threesome, and Buster, fell into a rhythm. Grace proved enormously helpful, having been something of a housekeeper for her father as well as cook and daughter. Paddy left after breakfast Friday morning, Kate's letters in his pocket. Buster settled into his guard post in the tiny front yard. Kate and Grace washed up and tidied the house, then readied a basket of fresh garden vegetables a churchwoman had brought by for a hearty soup.

Midday, Kate and Grace walked to the shop with Paddy's lunch, exchanging a few words with the shopkeepers and villagers they met on the streets. After he'd eaten, Paddy took the wagon out to make deliveries, and Kate kept shop with Grace as her assistant. Late that afternoon, Laura Peterman dropped in again, bringing her daughter, Elizabeth, and Kate readily agreed to Laura's suggestion that the girls walk down to the bay for a bit of fresh air. The two practically bounced as they headed out the door and down Front Street.

"Thank you," Kate said. "I'd hoped Grace would want to spend time with other girls her age, but she hadn't mentioned any friends and I'm too new in town to know all the adults, let alone their children."

"I'll confess, I wanted a moment with you," Laura said. "To ask how Grace is doing, and how you're holding up. But also to confirm a few things for the funeral service and the burial at Lone Pine."

Paddy had pointed out the cemetery, a few miles north of town, but she'd had no reason to visit yet. "It's a lovely spot, and the mountains are stunning, but—" Kate broke off, holding her hand to her heart. "Is it fanciful to think he might be lonely there, so far from the land where he was raised, and from his late wife's grave?"

"One is never alone, or lonely, when one accepts God's grace. As Reverend Haugen most surely did."

Kate sighed. "I only wish he'd designated someone to care for his daughter, if he died." Surely a man who frequently confronted human mortality would have thought about his daughter's future.

"I have the impression that there were family difficulties. As happens from time to time."

Would Kate's letter make those difficulties better or worse? Had she meddled where she ought not?

"The churchwomen will organize a picnic lunch after the burial," Laura continued. "Since the church hall is being used by the school right now, we can eat at the cemetery after the burial, if the weather holds, or plan to gather in the school, if you'd prefer."

She had no preference, no reason to have one. It was good of Laura Peterman to ask, out of courtesy for her temporary guardianship of the girl, but she had no idea what to do.

"Which would you choose?"

"I would choose a picnic on the cemetery lawn. It's the custom back East, and I've always enjoyed it."

"Where back East did you come from?" Kate wasn't good at identifying accents, probably because she'd been so few places herself.

"Pittsburgh," Laura said, after a brief hesitation. "Now, is there anything you need? Anything we can do for you?"

"Thank you, no. People have dropped by extra food, which I appreciate, though Grace doesn't eat much and we are grocers." Kate flashed a quick grin. "She'll be going back to school on Monday, and once we're in a routine . . ."

"Yes. Routines are good for children. But Sunday, after the service and lunch and all the excitement . . ." Laura's voice trailed off. "You should be prepared."

Kate took a deep breath and exhaled. Be prepared for tears, as the loss sunk in. "Thank you. You've been most kind."

Laura Peterman responded with a sweet, slightly sad smile, and bought a few sticks of candy before collecting the girls. Grace returned with a healthy flush on her cheeks and a lightness that gave Kate hope.

The rest of the day went smoothly, the whoosh of wheels and clack of hooves outside mingling with conversation and the jangle of the cash register inside. Saturday followed much the same pattern. There was no word of the thieves, or the second candlestick. Kate did not see Thaddeus London again, and she didn't mind. At home, in the evenings, she attempted to sew while Grace read to them, but she was not a good seamstress at the best of times, and her nerves were too jangled for delicate work right now. Later. There would be plenty of time later, in the long winter ahead.

In the front pew, Grace sitting straight-backed between her and Paddy, Kate tried to focus on the visiting minister's words. Tried to forget that he stood on the very spot where she had found Reverend Haugen on what the minister called "that unholy day." But how could she, the way the man went on about his dear, departed friend's faith and his love of Christ and his constant prayers for the soul of the community, and finally, a word about his love for his only child.

She could not, would not, forget that Arval Haugen had been a man first, and a father, and then a minister. His failure to consider Grace, should anything happen to him, was troubling. He had lost his wife; he knew better than most the dangers. He and his daughter had been cast out, if Grace had the story right, from the only family remaining. As Laura Peterman had said the other day in the shop, these things happen.

But she could not blame Reverend Haugen for not wanting to

believe he might die early. Surely he had expected there would be time to repair the relationship with his mother-in-law. For Grace's sake, and the love of his late wife.

After the service, a procession of automobiles, buggies, and wagons headed for the cemetery. Laura's recommendation had been a good one. The view of the mountains was magnificent and the minister's words mercifully brief before the six strong men, Paddy among them in a nod to his role in the community and to having taken in young Grace, even though he was a Catholic, lowered the casket into the grave.

Grace stood silently. After she had tossed a handful of rich, dark dirt onto the casket, she'd tucked her bare hand into Kate's gloved one and kept it there as the mourners filed by, paying their last respects. Grace accepted their condolences in a manner that suited her name, convincing Kate that Arval and Freya Haugen had been good parents, despite their feud with Mrs. Swensen.

And then Kate and Paddy were alone by the grave with Grace, the minister and sexton a few feet away.

"Shall we leave you here with your father for a bit?" Kate asked.

"No," Grace replied quickly. Then she knelt, the skirt of her dark brown dress just missing the fresh dirt around the edge of the grave. Folded her hands and bowed her head. Kate took Paddy's hand, and they waited.

Then the threesome picked their way down the slope to the sprawling lawn where the churchwomen had spread out quilts and opened their baskets. Kate hadn't brought a basket, having been told it wasn't necessary, but she wasn't immediately sure where to go. Anne Lang beckoned them, rising and giving her pupil a quick but firm embrace.

"Kate, I don't believe you've met my brother, Frank." Anne gestured to the young man who had pushed himself up with difficulty, his shoulders uneven, one leg several inches shorter than the other. "Frank, this is Mrs. Murphy."

"I've seen you in the post office," he said, holding out his hand.

"Your husband owns the Mercantile." Frank Lang's words were not easy to understand, and one side of his face drooped. But his grip was firm and his eyes were gentle.

"He does," she said. "Grace and I have been helping out this past week."

They settled on the yellow-and-white quilt, in the popular Flying Geese pattern. Paddy sat beside her a few minutes later, after the inevitable stops for a quick conversation. Anne passed around plates of ham and potato salad and poured glasses of lemonade. Ivan Gregory joined them, telling stories of the small towns where he'd worked before settling here. He kept it light, though Kate had heard enough from Paddy and the men in the Mercantile to know that conditions were sometimes quite dangerous, pay low, and bosses hard. Ivan Gregory did not seem like a hard boss, and she hoped that was true, particularly when she saw the effort he made to amuse Anne Lang and the flush on the teacher's cheeks. It was almost like a carefree summer picnic, despite the reason for the gathering, and Grace ate more than Kate had ever seen.

"There's Daniel Gibson," Paddy said to Kate. He handed her his plate and pushed himself up. "I'll go have a word."

Kate watched him go. She recognized several families from the shop or piano lessons. The Petermans sat not far away, Laura and James and their three children, and Laura waved. When she turned back to her own group, Gregory was relaying a story about a stubborn mule that had Grace and Frank captivated, but Anne's attention was elsewhere. Kate followed the teacher's gaze to where Paddy stood with Gibson, beside a graceful birch. Then the two men shook hands and Paddy moved on. The teacher kept watching the deputy sheriff, and Kate could not read the expression on her face as the man looked toward their quintet.

"I should go say hello to a few people, if you don't mind," Kate said when Gregory finished his story. "Grace, would you like to say hello to Elizabeth?"

Grace quickly agreed. They thanked Anne, said their goodbyes, and joined the Petermans, where Grace accepted a slice of cake and settled in next to her friend. Laura stood and walked a few feet away with Kate.

"This was an excellent recommendation," Kate said. "Thank you. It's good for Grace to see the community's respect for her father."

"He was a good man. I only wish—" She broke off, catching her lower lip between her teeth and clutching her elbows.

Kate did not dare ask what she wished. Then Laura took her hand and spoke fervently.

"You're young, Kate. And it's clear that you have a good heart, if an innocent one. Please, don't judge people for their mistakes. We all make them, and some . . . well, some mistakes simply can't be undone."

And with that, Laura Peterman squeezed her hand and returned to the colorful log cabin quilt where her family sat and began to pack up. Kate could not see her face. Perhaps, when Reverend Haugen had ridden his bicycle out to visit with the Petermans, he had told her about the rift with his late wife's mother. Yes, that was it—Laura had mentioned something of the family trouble when she'd been in the Mercantile.

Kate was relieved to know he'd found someone to confide in. How difficult it must be for men of the cloth to hear other people's concerns and not often have the chance to express their own.

"Mrs. Murphy," the mother of another piano student called. Kate greeted the woman and was introduced to her husband and other children. She wove her way through the gathering, hoping to remember new names and faces the next time they met. To her surprise, the atmosphere was quite pleasant, not maudlin at all. Perhaps that was because the town was too new for many graves. There would be more grief to come. Almost everyone shared a story about Reverend Haugen, and it seemed clear that he'd been well-liked, even loved. The doctor expressed his fervent wish that today's visiting minister would not be taking over the church in Jewel Bay, "or we'll all turn deaf, from him talking our ears off." Several women asked about Grace, and Kate had to acknowledge that she did not yet know what would happen to the girl.

But she had not grown up with three sisters without developing the ability to hear bits of conversation not meant for her. A shocking suggestion that Reverend Haugen might not have kept every secret as quiet as he should have. A comment that Ivan Gregory might now have the chance to buy the land he'd been coveting for his orchard, land some thought better for a new church and school. She needed a break from all the talk.

Pretend you're in Baraboo, she told herself. *Smile, say a few words, like Alice or your mother would do. And keep moving.*

When she reached the top of the cemetery, she paused to read the inscription beneath a stone lamb. An infant, dead at just three months.

"You there!" a rough male voice shouted, and Kate jerked her head up. Who could be yelling at her?

"What are you up to?" the man continued, his heavy forehead wrinkled, a thick hand waving. "He bothering you, miss?"

"Who?" Was he talking to her? She twisted her head and glimpsed Frank Lang, partially hidden by a large spruce, one of a row that marked the far edge of the cemetery. Frank was hurriedly buttoning his pants. "Oh, good heavens, no."

But the man ignored her protest and grabbed at Frank's arm. Frank tried to pull away, but with his poor balance, he stumbled and the man easily snared him.

"How do we know an imbecile like you didn't kill the reverend? We know he had a hankering to marry your sister. He'd have tossed you out on your ear," the man said. "Now here you are, making a pest of yourself with this young woman."

"I—I just came up—here to—to make water," Frank stammered.

"I don't know who you are," Kate said to the man, "but I'll thank you not to speak so rudely. Frank has done nothing wrong." A movement caught her eye and she spotted Daniel Gibson a short ways away.

"That's enough, Henry," Gibson said, stepping into the scene. "Mrs. Murphy says Frank wasn't bothering her, and we'll take her at her word."

"You should be looking at him for the murder," Henry said. "We all know it doesn't take much for a defect like him to turn violent."

"I know no such thing," Gibson replied as he led the man away.

Kate put her hand on her heart to slow it down. Frank had finished buttoning his pants and was watching her uncertainly.

"Are you all right, Frank? What a horrid man."

"He—he'd have hurt me if—if you hadn't stopped him. Thank you, Miss Ka—Kate."

"Shall we rejoin your sister?"

Frank nodded and they made their way down the hill. Frank walked slowly, planting one leg and swinging the other around, using his arms for balance. Kate stayed close, though she was too small to help much if he fell. It was plain that some folks had heard Henry's words and shared his distrust of Frank, while others had no idea what had happened.

How terrible that Frank, and Anne, had to endure such hatred. How widespread was it? Was Jewel Bay, despite its name, not as polished or genteel a town as its leading residents might want to think? Was Paddy right to believe in the town's promise? Could a town where thieves went uncaught and murder—in a church, no less—went unsolved prosper and thrive? Should they pull up stakes while they could?

If they could.

No. It was impossible. Paddy had sunk everything into this town—his money, his heart, and his hopes. And on a day so bright and clear, how could she not believe, too—even if they were gathered for the funeral of a well-loved man. Even if there were gossips and cruel tongues amid the offers of spare clothing for Grace, and a cot that could be folded up and tucked out of the way. This was the town they had chosen. The town where they had cast their lot and their luck.

They reached Anne's quilt and Frank thanked her again before settling himself next to his sister. Should she mention the incident? Then an arm slipped around her waist and the touch and scent of Paddy Murphy enveloped her. She buried her head in his shoulder. A silent sob wracked her and he held her close.

"Ah, lass," he whispered. "You're safe with me."

Was she safe? Was Grace? Oh, how she wanted to believe it.

"Paddy," she said when they were alone that night in their bedroom, "is it true that Reverend Haugen wanted to marry Anne Lang? What would have happened to Frank?"

Paddy's eyes went wide as he unbuttoned his shirt, the collar hanging loose around his neck.

"News to me, lass. Where's this coming from?"

She told him about the incident in the cemetery.

"Henry Clyde," Paddy said, his eyes darkening. "It's him you got to be watching out for."

"Was the reverend courting Anne?"

"Mighta been. I'd say if she's partial to anyone, it's Ivan Gregory."

That made sense. Anne had invited him to sit with them, after all, and they'd chatted easily. It had been Anne who suggested Ivan take the reverend's bicycle for his nephew, who ran errands for the power company, since it was too big for Grace.

Kate unpinned her hair and reached for her brush. "She is attractive, and there aren't many unmarried women of a suitable age in town."

Paddy tossed his collar on top of the dresser and wriggled out of his shirt. "Sounds to me like you did as much watching as you did listening."

"I could hardly help it, could I? Tell me about your conversation with the deputy. Does he think Frank Lang might have turned violent? I can't believe it. I sat with them for nearly an hour and Frank seems as gentle a man as there is."

"Oh, aye. And I don't mean to be sharp with you. Frank talks slow and moves poorly, but he's right enough in the head. Can't say the same for Henry Clyde."

"He didn't like me setting him straight, that's for sure. I expect that's one customer we've lost."

"And one we don't need," Paddy answered. "But you know how cruel people can be about those who look different."

They were both thinking, Kate knew, about a man back home who'd been kicked in the head by a horse, leaving him with one eye and a misshapen skull. He'd done no harm to anyone, but a group of older boys had been merciless, mistreating him to the point that town elders had intervened and put a stop to it.

"I think they're scared," he continued. "Because they don't understand, and they know it could happen to any of us."

Kate finished brushing her hair and began to braid it for the night. "Do you know what happened to Frank?"

"School board hired Anne on the recommendation of a woman in Pondera, and when she arrived with Frank in tow, it went about that he'd been injured in the same train wreck that killed their parents. I've never had any reason to doubt it. He would have been a boy, though I'd put him at twenty-one or -two by now. He does odd jobs around town— feeding stock, stacking wood. But it can't amount to much."

If he couldn't support himself, then he was a burden. If that limited Anne's marriage possibilities, did she mind? It was hard to imagine Ivan Gregory resenting a crippled brother, and as manager of the power plant, surely he could afford to support his wife's relative, especially one who could work around the house. If they were right about Ivan's interest, and if Anne returned it.

Stacking wood, Paddy had said. Gibson and his men had taken the woodpile apart but hadn't found the second candlestick. Where could it be?

"There must be something we can do," Kate said. "To stop the awful talk."

"Lass, what a heart you've got. But let the questions go." Paddy pulled back the bedcovers and held out an arm. His eyes danced in the lamplight and his lips curved. "Come to bed."

And she happily did.

∞

Monday. A clean slate, full of promise, her mother always said. And this Monday was both. Kate decided to walk Grace to school, since it was her first day back, and on the way, they chatted about lessons and the books Miss Lang had lent her, already finished.

Children swarmed the school from all directions, alone or in clusters. They shouted, laughed, and taunted each other, and Kate relished the sound.

"Grace!" Elizabeth Peterman called. Grace waved back, then glanced at Kate.

"Go on then," Kate said. "After school, wait for me outside and we'll walk home together."

Grace flashed her a smile and ran to her friend.

"Good to have her back," a woman said. Anne Lang. The two women watched the girls, Grace showing Elizabeth the borrowed books, the pair chatting happily. "She seems to be coping well."

"Most of the time," Kate said. "It's a big loss for a girl who's already suffered a serious blow."

"I was much older than Grace when our parents were killed. Almost twenty-one. But Frank was so young, and I left teachers' college to take care of him."

"A big responsibility to take on, at a hard time. How did you decide to come to Montana?"

"Not so much a decision," Anne said, "as the only option we had. The president of the college took a special interest in finding a placement for me and wrote to an alumna who lives in Pondera. She arranged a position, even though I hadn't finished my training. But when we arrived, I discovered that there was no opening after all."

"Oh, my. That must have been devastating. What happened?"

"I never knew whether the woman I was to replace ended her engagement, or something happened to her intended. The school board allowed her to rescind her resignation, which was the right thing to do, but it left me at loose ends."

One generosity becoming another's hardship. It was unfair that a woman could not teach after she married, a subject of much debate among the females in the Flannery household, especially after Kate's sister, Mary, chose a teaching career, but it was almost universally true.

"We were fortunate," Anne continued, "that Jewel Bay needed a teacher and was willing to overlook the unusual circumstances."

Which no doubt included Frank. But Kate wasn't going to ask about him.

"I'd like to hear," Kate said, choosing her words with care, "your thoughts on a long-term situation for Grace. If no relatives step forward. I've written to her grandmother, though from what Grace has said, a welcome seems unlikely."

One of the older boys rang the bell, and the children began to form lines by grade, girls in front, boys in back.

"No, not a happy tale, I'm afraid," Anne replied. "I'm sure you'll hear, if you haven't already, rumors about Arval Haugen and me. About marriage."

"I—" Kate raised her hands in protest.

"No. I want you to know. We did take a few walks together, down along the bay. Ate a picnic supper by the ferry landing. Arval was a good man. I would have married him, if he'd asked."

If.

"But he never did. He was burdened by the sense that marrying again would betray his late wife."

Better, Kate supposed, than treating marriage as a transaction or convenience. But given the risks of the world, a view that condemned one to loneliness, and denied the heart a second chance.

"I'm sure you'll have other opportunities," Kate said. "An attractive single woman, in a town with a lot of single men . . . I'd say Ivan Gregory has his eye on you. And maybe Daniel Gibson, too."

"What is it that makes every married woman think every single woman desires the same state?" Anne Lang said in a tone that could be joking or serious. The bell rang again and she bustled off.

Kate watched her usher the children into the school and wondered what bucket of mire she had stepped into.

On her way down to the Mercantile late that morning, she again saw Thaddeus London walking near Ivan Gregory's two-story yellow house. The man said nothing, though he tipped his head and lifted his cap. She'd ask Paddy about him later. She asked a lot of questions, but that was the best way to get to know the townspeople, and as Paddy often said, he knew everyone because everyone needed potatoes and nails.

On Mondays, Paddy did not make deliveries, but there was plenty of custom, so Kate stayed until it was time for piano lessons.

"You're a quick learner, lass," Paddy said, and his compliment made her warm inside.

The week grew long. No sign of the suspected thieves was reported and no arrests were made. A thin fog of fear had settled over the town, which Kate hated. She did not want to live like that, but nor did she want Grace to go on without knowing the truth about her father's death. Even if it was harsh, more than an eleven-year-old ought to have to bear. It did no good to hide the truth from children and claim you were protecting them.

One evening, Grace took the embroidery hoop from Kate's hands.

"Let me show you." She made a length of backstitches then a graceful sweep of stem stitches, making sure Kate watched closely. "Now you try."

"How did you learn to embroider so beautifully?" Kate asked as she took the linen and loop.

"My mother taught me."

Every night, Paddy helped Grace set up the cot behind the sofa. It was a good solution, but a temporary one—a growing girl could not sleep forever on a borrowed cot in the front room. More than once, Kate heard her crying quietly. Sometimes she steeled herself against the tears and let her be, but other times, she put a hand on the quivering back and the girl threw her thin arms around Kate and sobbed.

One afternoon midweek, Kate finished her lesson with Elizabeth Peterman and went outside with the girl. Grace sat on a bench reading and keeping an eye on Elizabeth's younger brother and sister. A canvas satchel lay open on the ground, papers sliding out, and Kate picked them up. One was a drawing of a man in a cap, arm raised, mouth open, a woman close by. Behind them stood a large house with columns flanking the front door and a tall leafy tree.

A chill rippled up her spine. Did these bright, lively children with their beautiful mother, their prosperous father, and their elegant home, live in the shadow of violence?

"Oh, Mrs." Young James, seven or eight, ran up. "That's mine."

Kate handed him the satchel but held on to the picture. "Did you draw this?"

"Yes. We were supposed to draw a visitor. It's a man who came to see my mother last week."

"It's not your father? I mean, the man in the picture."

"Oh, no. He never gets angry. Not with our mother, anyway. He was angry when he heard about the man who came to visit, though."

"I should think so. Do you know who the man was, or what he and your mother were talking about?"

"No. I was in the tree, way high up. Too high to hear them. I am very good at climbing trees."

Kate handed back the drawing. "I can tell. What did your teacher say about your picture?"

"She never got to me. She only looks at the good drawings, and I'm not very good."

"I like to draw. Maybe we can draw together sometime."

"It's okay," he said. "I'd rather climb trees."

But his drawing had been good enough to convey the man's anger and the woman's fear, Kate thought. Then the children's father drove up and they ran to the Packard. The house was a long walk, even without concern about thieves, and it was no wonder Reverend Haugen had used his bicycle to visit the Petermans. But it was not Reverend Haugen in the drawing. The boy would have known him, and despite his lack of skill with the wax crayon, would have added the reverend's distinctive hat.

Who would assail the kind and gentle Mrs. Peterman? Why? And what had James Peterman done, when he heard the story from his wife?

"Grace," Kate said as the two walked home. "Has Elizabeth ever said anything to you about her parents arguing? Or about a man making threats?"

But Grace said no, and Kate let the matter drop.

On Friday, five days after Reverend Arval Haugen's burial, a letter arrived from Chicago. Paddy left it for Kate, propped on the brass cash register, and she took it up to his private office to read.

> *Mrs. Murphy,*
>
> *Thank you for your letter with news of the misfortune that has struck Mr. Haugen. How distressing it must have been to find him. You will think me cold for lacking much sympathy for the man, and perhaps I am. I have not yet forgiven him, despite the passage of time, for putting my daughter into the impoverished condition that led to her death. By serving God, you will say. No. By his insistence on doing so despite knowing that she was fragile, that working in the slums amid filth and poverty would expose her to disease. By allowing his belief that God had destined him to bring the comfort of Christ to the poor and the immigrants to outweigh his responsibilities as a husband and father.*

There it was, the barest acknowledgment of her granddaughter. But the woman went on, continuing her description of the vile conditions of those Reverend Haugen had ministered to, and her rage over her daughter's death. Her anger, Kate could understand. It was part of grief. Consumption was a horrible disease, but it could have struck Freya Haugen anywhere. Even in her mother's wealthy neighborhood. Even here, with all the fresh air one could breathe. And why blame him? It was clear that he had suffered deeply, even letting his loss keep him from the possibility of new happiness.

In conclusion, she wrote, *if there is no one else willing to take the girl, you may send her to me. I am sure there are those among my acquaintance who can make arrangements.*

"Arrangements?" Kate spat out the word. "We're talking about a child, not a garden party. Your flesh and blood, Mrs. Agnete Swensen of Chicago. And I am not sending an eleven-year-old girl halfway across the country on a train by herself."

Paddy would help her figure out what to do. She dried her eyes and started down the stairs, the gray linen envelope in hand. At the sound of a man speaking in the hallway, she stopped.

"It's this business about Arval Haugen, Paddy," the man said. "It's shaking things up. People are talking about leaving town, pulling up stakes."

"Not you, James," she heard Paddy say. James Peterman? "Not with all you've done to establish the bank. The investments you've made."

Among them, the loan that had financed the Mercantile.

"We'll have to see, Paddy. We'll have to see. But it would be better, don't you agree, if we all acknowledged that the murder occurred in the course of a theft, and left off asking questions?"

Kate froze, her hand over her mouth. He was talking about her. James Peterman must have heard from his son that she'd asked about the drawing, about who he'd seen and what he'd heard. James Peterman wanted her to stop asking questions and—he'd made this clear by his tone as well as his words—if she didn't, he would withdraw his support for the Mercantile. The shop that was Paddy's heart and dream.

She could not hear Paddy's reply over the thumping in her chest. Not until she heard two sets of footsteps heading back to the shop floor did she dare to breathe again. When she was sure they had gone and could not hear her move, she retreated to the office under the eaves.

Had the boy pretended that the man he'd drawn was a visitor, not wanting to admit it was a picture of his father shouting at his mother? Secure in the knowledge that the teacher would not inspect his drawing, had the boy drawn the violence he'd seen, knowing no one would ever guess the truth? Until she'd picked up the wrinkled paper, smoothed it out, and asked him about it.

Or the man, not much more than a stick figure, might have been Reverend Haugen after all, the boy unable to see him clearly from his leafy perch.

Or what if—and this sent a chill down her spine as cold as the Baraboo River in the dead of winter—what if James Peterman, by all accounts as good-natured as he was prosperous, had himself been involved in the reverend's murder?

She could not stay up here all afternoon, and she couldn't sneak out the back door. Paddy would worry, and troubled as she was, she would not add to her husband's burden. Besides, they truly did have to decide what to do about Mrs. Swensen's letter, and Grace.

Thank goodness Paddy was alone, polishing the perfectly clean counter with a thick white cloth. At the sound of her footsteps, he raised his head, his hand stopping mid-swirl. His face was pale, his hair mussed.

His Adam's apple bobbed. "There yeh are, lass. Bad news then?"

She gestured with the envelope. "How could a woman as horrid as Mrs. Swensen raise such a loving wife and mother as Freya Haugen?"

"Kate, you know she's acting out of her grief, first over her daughter's decision to marry against her wishes, and then over her death."

"It's been years, Paddy. Why can't she put her grief aside for the sake of her granddaughter? The granddaughter whose love and comfort she has denied herself, out of her own bitterness." Kate's own parents had not approved of every decision their daughters had made. They'd worried about Alice's intended before their marriage because his father had been known to strike his wife and children. But he'd proven himself a good provider and a devoted husband and father. They'd worried that Mary's decision to teach doomed her to a life alone, though Kate suspected that was what Mary wanted. They'd only agreed to let Margaret go to art school in Chicago because the school kept a private boardinghouse for its female students and did not allow men and women to study together until they reached advanced levels.

And her own decision to marry a man who was building a future hundreds of miles away had not been easy to accept.

Chicago. She couldn't ask her younger sister to visit Mrs. Swensen—the old lady would not take a young unmarried woman seriously. But what about Alice or Mrs. Flannery? They were mature women, mothers themselves, though Alice wasn't thirty yet and her children small. But she had a persuasive manner, and if the two women took the train together, to visit Margaret, maybe they could pay a call.

"It isn't right," Paddy said, "though I can see how Freya would have wanted to get away from her mother."

She must have been torn, but she'd chosen her husband, as she should. She'd chosen to make her own future. As Kate had.

Kate felt a battle of her own right now, between her fear that she'd put their future in danger, and her conviction that Reverend Haugen was murdered not by thieves but by someone right here in Jewel Bay.

One of their neighbors. A hot, sour taste filled her throat.

What if she was right? What if she was wrong?

But she had to put those feelings aside and focus on young Grace. She was just about to ask Paddy what he thought about enlisting her mother and Alice when the door opened. Paddy tucked the corner of his towel into his apron pocket. Kate straightened her spine and readied her face to welcome their customer.

But their visitor was not there to order supplies.

"Paddy," Deputy Gibson said. "Mrs. Murphy."

"Aye, Daniel." Paddy put out his hand and the men shook. "What's bringing you into the Mercantile today?"

"Is there any news?" Kate asked. "About the murder?"

The deputy deflected her question. "Mrs. Murphy, might I ask you to tell me more about that altercation in the cemetery?"

She glanced at Paddy, who gave her an encouraging nod. She'd told him everything Sunday night, so he wasn't surprised by the details, or the language, but she could see the protective glower drop over his face.

"I know the man," Gibson said after she wrapped up her story. "Farms north of town, by the river bend. I suspect his wife dragged him to Sunday services."

"Why are you asking, Daniel?" Paddy said. "Has something happened?"

"Yes, but it doesn't involve Henry Clyde. We've found the second silver candlestick."

"Where?" Kate and Paddy spoke at the same time.

Daniel Gibson rubbed his unshaven cheek.

"In Ivan Gregory's woodpile." He trained his steady gaze on Kate. "A pile he hired Frank Lang to stack."

Kate was grateful to have no students that afternoon. She knew she ought to go see Anne Lang, but feared her presence would be unwelcome, even though she'd done her best to intervene when Henry Clyde confronted Frank. Though Gibson had questioned Frank, he had not arrested him. He'd told his boss that he couldn't spare the time from his other duties to haul him thirty miles to the jail in Pondera. The real reason, he'd told Kate and Paddy, was that Frank's stammer and limp and the accusation that he'd killed a man of the cloth would make him an easy target of the other prisoners.

How long he could keep Frank out of jail, Gibson hadn't wanted to guess. Most likely, the sheriff would overrule the decision, even though Frank's damaged leg meant he couldn't escape without help. Even so, the delay was a relief. Kate didn't know if Gibson possessed a tender side she had not seen until now, or was motivated by his admiration for Anne.

Did it matter why you did the right thing, as long as you did it?

She'd stayed in the shop the rest of the afternoon, helping Paddy, though both were subdued. A few customers had heard the news and offered their theories. Why, one wondered, had Gregory hired Frank to stack the wood, a job his nephew could have done? So the boy could focus on his schoolwork, Kate supposed, since that was the reason he spent the week in town. Plenty of work to do on weekends at his parents' homestead. She'd almost bitten her tongue half through when a man in a dirty coverall said, "That's the thanks you get for hiring an idiot." Paddy, bless him, had told the man to take his purchases and leave.

By unspoken agreement, Kate and Paddy said nothing when Grace arrived after school, smiling, with a new book a teacher had lent her. Not Miss Lang, who had been absent this afternoon. Kate offered the girl her choice from the penny candy jars, and she chose a long stick of hard candy, which turned her tongue purple.

Not until they were home did Kate tell her about the discovery of the candlestick and the fear that Frank Lang had killed her father.

"But that can't be," Grace protested. "Frank respected my father. He helped out at the church whenever he could, making small repairs or stacking wood."

"To some, that means Frank would have known exactly how and where to hide the candlesticks."

Grace's hands flew to her mouth. "But why? Why would he do that?"

"I don't believe it either. But people are ready to think the worst of him because of his condition." Kate paused, wanting to get the words right. "Some think Frank knew of your father's fondness for Anne and feared that if she married him, he, Frank, would be left on his own."

"Miss Lang would never have done that! Papa would never have wanted her to!"

Kate was surprised. "Did your father speak to you about Miss Lang?"

"Not in that way," Grace said, her pale cheeks pinking. "But he enjoyed her company, and I thought he might want to marry her. She would have been a wonderful mother, I think, as good as my real mother. And Papa was the kindest, gentlest soul, Kate. He would never have thrown Frank out."

Kate believed her. And she did not believe Frank Lang had killed Arval Haugen. Not over his sister, and not over a useless pair of silver candlesticks.

She stood and crossed to the stove, where she picked up a heavy wooden spoon and stirred the soup, its fragrance filling the tiny space. Besides, if Frank Lang had taken the candlesticks, wouldn't he have hidden them more carefully?

Had the killer wanted the single candlestick to be found? Why? And why leave the other in Ivan Gregory's woodpile? So it could be found, too?

She used the edge of the spoon to pry bits of ham off the bone.

One thing she knew for sure: something, and someone, in Jewel Bay was not as it appeared to be.

"Ah, Kate. You know I love your big heart. But she belongs with her people," Paddy said as they sat at the kitchen table after supper. Grace had taken Buster outside, then settled down to read in the front room.

"Even if they don't want her? What will happen if that bitter old woman dies? Paddy, think about the dangers a young girl, a young woman on her own faces in this world. At best, she'd be farmed out as a servant and at worst . . . I'll find her a home myself before I commit her to that fate."

"We've got our own future to think about. Our own family."

"You always say that the Irish make room at the table, even if it means one less mouthful for those already there."

Paddy pressed his lips together. "Aye, lass, yeh got me there. But it's a big decision. Let's not rush it."

Maybe he was right. She wasn't sure anymore.

Not until after both Paddy and Grace had gone to bed was Kate able to sit with a cup of tea and the letter from Alice, nearly forgotten in the confusion created by Mrs. Swensen's screed and the conversation she'd overheard between Paddy and James Peterman.

My dearest Kate, Alice wrote in a strong, clear hand. *How wrenching to find that poor man.* After expressing her sympathy for his daughter and concern for Kate, she assured Kate that she would not reveal "the lurid details" to their mother.

> *Never hesitate, little sister, to unburden yourself to me. Even the heaviest load is lighter when shared, and you are wise to grasp that there will be matters you do not want to share with your husband, good man that he is, for fear of worrying him.*

Alice went on to talk about the family, including the latest antics of her children, five-year-old William and three-year-old Frances.

As for the girl and her grandmother, Alice wrote in closing, *that is a heartbreaking situation. No family is everything we want it to be. You must consider your decision long and hard, as I know you will, and be guided by your generous spirit.*

Easy to say, Kate thought as she folded the letter and slid it back into the ivory envelope, her sister's initials engraved on the back. Not so easy to do.

The next morning, Kate knew what she needed to do.

"I can walk to school by myself," Grace said when Kate untied her apron.

"I know you can. But I need to speak with Miss Lang."

Anne Lang was at her post when Kate, Grace, and Buster arrived, and if the woman's shoulders stiffened at the sight of them, Kate could not blame her. Did she suspect Kate of pointing the finger, after the altercation in the cemetery? Kate wanted Anne to know that she had not accused Frank, and to assure her that Daniel Gibson was not her brother's only friend in Jewel Bay.

"Anne. May I have a word?" The other woman hesitated briefly before drawing Kate aside. "Deputy Gibson told us about the discovery of the second candlestick, and that there are those who believe it proves Frank killed Reverend Haugen. They are fools."

Anne gripped her elbows, tightened her lips, and waited.

"I've told him everything that happened in the cemetery. How the farmer accused Frank of following me, mocking and taunting him when he had trouble replying. I made clear then, and again yesterday to Deputy Gibson, that Frank was blameless. That it was I who had startled him, when I came around the big tree at the top of the cemetery and found him—" Kate willed herself not to blush like a schoolgirl. "Well, there is no outhouse and sometimes a man can't wait."

Anne's lips twitched.

"My mind's been spinning ever since the deputy's visit, and the more I've thought about it, the more convinced I am that Frank could not have killed Reverend Haugen."

"But how can we prove it? Henry Clyde is not the first man to spread rumors about my brother. Frank swears he was sitting by the river all afternoon the day Arval was killed, listening to the birds. He often does—birds have always fascinated him. But no one saw him," Anne said, her voice breaking.

"When we were walking down the hill in the cemetery," Kate said, "I noticed how Frank has to set one leg as a brace, when the ground is uneven, then swing the other leg around. He holds out his arms to steady himself." She demonstrated.

"Yes," Anne said. "The injury affected his balance. That's one reason he can't work a regular job, or a full shift."

And one reason why people feared him. His movements appeared menacing, but Kate had seen how they took every bit of his concentration.

"Ivan Gregory was being generous," Anne continued, "paying Frank to stack the wood. He and his nephew cut and split it—Frank can't swing an axe that long. But stacking is work he can do, even with his damaged leg and his twisted shoulders."

"The reverend was hit and killed on the altar," Kate said. The early bell rang. "Frank couldn't have stepped up onto the altar without grabbing the altar table to steady himself, could he?"

"No."

"And he couldn't have grabbed the candlestick and hit the reverend. He'd have lost his balance, even before taking a swing. The reverend wasn't old, and he was fit. He walked or bicycled everywhere. And he knew Frank's infirmities."

"He knew Frank was no threat to him," Anne said. "Have you told Daniel Gibson this? I am convinced he wants to believe Frank innocent, but it's difficult. So many people are willing to believe Frank guilty just because he's different."

"I'll tell him. Let's hope he's willing to believe a young woman." She hesitated, knowing they didn't have much time for the other topic on her mind. "Anne, I've heard from Grace's grandmother. As you predicted, her response bordered on the cruel. I wish I could ask you to take the girl—she admires you so. But I know you can't. It wouldn't be seemly, not with an unmarried man in the house. Especially not now, with all that's happened."

"The second bell's about to ring," Anne said, stretching out a hand, not quite touching Kate's arm. "My mentor in Pondera might be able to make a place for Grace, but I would hate to uproot her from her friends and school right now. Kate, are you sure you can't keep her?" Then, without waiting for an answer, the teacher swept toward the students, hands in the air, calling out greetings.

How could they keep her? They had no room in their tiny log refuge, and Kate was too young to mother a girl Grace's age. But family, it seemed, though the thought broke every rule in Kate's heart, was not always the best place for a child.

As the children processed into the building, she saw Grace pair up with Elizabeth. What about the Petermans? Laura appeared to be an excellent mother and had a daughter Grace's age, as well as a large house. But not if there were violence in the home.

Back at their own house, she was surprised to find a basket at the front door. It was lined with a linen towel, beautifully embroidered, and held jars of apple jelly and strawberry jam, a brown paper packet of tea, and a box of French milled soap studded with lavender. A small ivory envelope bore her name.

Inside, Kate refilled Buster's water dish and sat to read the note.

My dear Mrs. Murphy, it began. *Thank you for your kindness toward my son, James, Jr., outside the school on Wednesday afternoon. What he lacks in drawing skill, he makes up for in imagination. His head is so filled with tales that I think he might well be our next Mr. Twain or Mr. Baum.*

Mr. Twain had been a favorite in the Flannery household, and they had all been saddened by his death last spring. Mr. Baum's novels, they had not enjoyed so much.

> *It was good of you to tolerate his antics, and as he is only seven, I trust you will not take him too seriously.*
> *Yours most sincerely,*
> *Laura Peterman*

Kate sat back. The dog had finished his drink and sat beside her. She stroked his head and peered into his deep brown eyes.

"What do you think, Buster? She's telling me not to be concerned.

But why me? We've just met. Which makes me more concerned."

Adding a person to the household made more work, and Kate was busy all morning. She again spent the afternoon helping customers while Paddy made his rounds. Talk had turned back to the murder and to Frank Lang, with half the town convinced he was the killer and that Daniel Gibson knew it; his failure to make the arrest clearly meant he was a victim of Anne Lang's charms; and what had Ivan Gregory been thinking, hiring a man like Frank, though some of the words used were far too unkind for Kate to repeat, even to herself. The other half would have sworn on a stack of Bibles that the poor soul was as innocent as a newborn lamb and thank goodness Daniel Gibson had a good heart as well as a good head. More than one wondered if Ivan Gregory himself didn't warrant a second look. Why a prosperous man would have stolen the candlesticks and hidden them in woodpiles, no one could explain, but it must have had something to do, the theory went, with Gregory coveting land meant for higher purposes for his orchard. Or his fear that the reverend would beat him to the altar with Anne Lang.

As if, Kate thought in disgust, that capable woman were a ball to be batted back and forth between men, her beloved brother nothing more than a hindrance.

A shopkeeper, Paddy had told her more than once, must not let on that he thinks his customers full of blarney. When they came into the Mercantile, they expected to have their say. Let any argument come from other customers, he'd said. Talk was their sport. Let them have it.

And so she did, keeping her head down and her tongue in her mouth, to use her mother's phrase.

Kate did not give lessons on Friday afternoons, so Grace was to walk down the hill with the postmaster's daughter, a year older, after school. When she didn't arrive, Kate took advantage of a quiet moment in the shop to dash across the street. The other girl had waited, then decided Grace must have left without her and walked down alone. It was perfectly safe, she said, casting her eyes sideways at her father. Busy with a customer, the man did not comment, but Kate understood the gesture. Until the killer was caught, or until Frank Lang was arrested, the opinion was that young girls were not safe on their own in this town.

And no town could prosper under that cloud.

But when Grace did not appear, Kate's own fears grew. Paddy returned and listened to her fret, then replied in his reassuring way, "We'll find her at the parsonage, as you did the other day, or back at the house, petting the dog, plumb forgetting she was meant to come to the shop."

But Grace was not a forgetful girl, or a disobedient one, and the knot in Kate's stomach did not loosen. They climbed in the Model T and motored up the hill. Grace was not at the parsonage. She was not at home, and the dog could not tell them if she had been there. Her school satchel was not where she usually left it, with her other things.

"Either she's run off, or somethin's happened to her," Paddy said.

That wise, practical Paddy would voice such fears made the knot tighten. If Grace had run off, she'd have come here first, knowing the house would be empty, to pack her little bag with clothing and her hairbrush and the photo of her mother, still on the side table where Kate had placed it.

"We'll take the automobile back down to the Mercantile and telephone Daniel Gibson."

"Let's check one more place," Kate pleaded.

But the surprise on Laura Peterman's face when she opened the door of the big white house overlooking the lake dashed Kate's hopes. Grace had not gone home with her friend.

Quickly, Kate explained their presence. Laura invited them in and called for her daughter. Elizabeth was tall for her age, taller than Kate, and though still girlish in build, promised to be both strong and elegant, like her mother. But she had not seen Grace since school let out. Had not seen what direction Grace had gone and had no idea where she might be. Kate sensed no deceit. Whatever Grace's plans, she had not confided them to her friend.

Kate sighed and glanced away from mother and daughter, wondering what to do next. The coin purse Kate had first seen in the Mercantile when Laura took it out to pay for the children's candy lay on the marble-topped hall table. The monogram reminded her of the basket and note.

"Forgive me," she said. "I nearly forgot to thank you for your gift. Did you embroider the towel yourself? I confess, the art has escaped me."

"I do enjoy needlework," Laura said. "Creating a bit of beauty from something plain."

Though the note had been intended to tamp down any concerns Kate might have of violence in the household, it had kindled them. But she could not ask the woman if she were safe, even obliquely, in the girl's presence, and not now, when more immediate matters pressed.

"Mama embroidered the altar cloths for the church," Elizabeth said. "Reverend Haugen called them the most beautiful handwork he'd seen, even better than his own wife's."

"Hush, child. We'll not boast in front of Mrs. Murphy," Laura said. But the compliment clearly pleased her.

Church work, then, had been one reason for the reverend's visits. Had Laura confided her situation to the minister? Had he known she was in danger in her home? Had he helped her form a plan to leave her husband and take her children to safety? Had James found out, become enraged, confronted Reverend Haugen and killed him?

Talk about imagination. And yet, it did happen, even in well-off families and gracious homes.

Her gaze settled on the monogrammed purse. *LLC*, though Laura's married name began with a *P*. Perhaps it had belonged to Laura's mother or another older relative, passed down after death. Kate's mother didn't carry one, but that didn't mean they weren't fashionable for that generation as well. Surely there was some explanation.

Her thoughts were disrupted by James Peterman, ushering Paddy through the front door. At the sound of their father's arrival, the two younger children emerged from elsewhere in the house, and they joined Elizabeth in greeting him. No mistaking their happiness.

Laura, too, had brightened. There was nothing fearful or guarded about the woman when she looked at her husband. No hesitation, only love and trust. Kate had been wrong. But that drawing, and the note . . .

She felt Laura's gaze on her and met it. It asked her—and she knew this; it was not imagination—to keep her secret. What was the secret? And why did it matter so much?

In the meantime, they had to find Grace.

"I'll telephone Gibson and we'll get up a search party," James Peterman was saying as Laura instructed Elizabeth to take the younger children to the kitchen and keep them occupied. "He must have some idea where that band of scoundrels is holed up."

He was voicing Kate's worst fear, that whoever had killed Reverend Haugen had come back for Grace. But who, and why?

"I think . . ." Kate said, hesitating.

"Out with it, lass," Paddy said.

"I think Grace may have heard us last night, talking about sending her to her grandmother. Then this morning, at the school, I talked with Anne Lang about finding a place for her. What if she overheard, or guessed that's what we were discussing, and that's why she's run off?" Too upset to gather up her few things first.

Laura gasped, and her husband slipped an arm around her.

It was quickly decided that while James summoned Deputy Gibson, Paddy and Kate would make another search of the familiar places. Perhaps there had been a misunderstanding. Perhaps Grace was fearful and hiding in the parsonage, or hungry, waiting in the Murphys' kitchen.

Not much of a plan. But what else could they do?

As they drove, a whirlwind of thoughts whipped through Kate's head. About Grace and her father. About James and Laura Peterman. Both husband and wife had consulted the reverend, who had also visited their home. Had Laura reached the same conclusion as Kate, after hearing him in the Mercantile with Paddy, that James had been involved in the reverend's death?

As they drove above the lakeshore, Kate frowned. "Paddy, that smoke down on the lakeshore. Is that the Indian encampment?" Grace had spoken more than once about visiting the Indians with her father.

"Aye, lass. Ohhh." He slowed and steered the Model T onto a trail so steep and rocky Kate found herself gripping the door as the wheels bounced and the automobile lurched from side to side.

At a wide spot, Paddy stopped. "We'll walk the rest of the way. Can you make it, lass, or should I be going down alone? It's ankle-spraining ground."

"Paddy Murphy, you are not leaving me here. If there's a chance Grace is with those Indians or they might know where she is, I don't care if I sprain my head!"

The trail narrowed, flattening as it reached the lakeshore. A man Paddy knew waited for them; no doubt he'd seen their headlamps. By the water's edge, a campfire blazed. Kate squinted in the last bit of daylight, searching, searching . . .

And there she was. A mix of relief and anger nearly overwhelmed Kate. She ran across the rocky shore and wrapped her arms around the girl.

"Grace! We were so frightened." Hands on the girl's shoulders, Kate searched her face in the firelight. Clearly, Grace had been frightened, too.

"Don't send me back," she pleaded. "Please. I'd rather be on my own, or be a servant, or anything but go where I'm not wanted."

"Oh, child." Kate pulled her close. "You're not going anywhere you don't want to go."

They thanked the families for tending to Grace for a few hours and the Indian man led them up the trail. Grace carried her satchel. Paddy guided the automobile up the hill, only cursing twice. Then he drove back to the Petermans to let them know the lost lamb had been found. They declined the offer of a hot drink by the fire, though when Laura suggested Grace spend Saturday with them, Kate readily agreed. With all the people who came into Jewel Bay to pick up groceries and tend to other errands, Saturday was Gossip Day, and with the discovery of the second candlestick and the focus on Frank Lang, tongues would be wagging. Grace did not need to hear the idle talk.

And Kate would find a moment, and a way, to speak with Laura alone. They had much to discuss.

Back in the Murphy kitchen, the fire in the cookstove crackling and the kettle on, Kate wished she could ask her mother or Alice for advice. How could she keep her promise to Grace?

First things first. Keep her warm and feed her, though she had been well treated down at the lakeshore. Kate had made her remove her boots and stockings and change into a dry dress—her school dress had gotten dirty and damp as she'd made her way through the brambles and undergrowth to the lakeshore.

Now she sat on the floor, hugging the dog. In her clean dress.

But it was good to see her acting like a child, this young girl who'd been forced to grow up too soon. She needed a place where she could run and play with other children, and without fear.

Kate set a steaming mug of coffee in front of Paddy and filled her teapot with hot water. The way she was going through the tea, she'd have to speak to him about ordering a decent supply sooner rather than later. Thank goodness for the small packet Laura had given her.

As if knowing the time for play had ended and the time for talk begun, Grace rose and sat in the third chair, the one they had stopped at the parsonage to fetch on the drive home.

"Did you have a plan, girl?" Paddy asked gently. "Or were you so set on getting away?"

"No! No. You've both been so good to me. I—" Grace bit her lip. "I'm sorry. I heard what you two said last night, and then the way you were talking to Miss Lang, Kate—I knew I couldn't go back to Chicago, but I never meant to worry you."

Kate squeezed her hand. "We know that. But we need to talk about your future. Miss Lang has a friend in Pondera, the woman who arranged for her to teach here. She has a lovely home not far from the county high school, and a grand piano and—"

"Can't I stay here? With the two of you? I don't mind sleeping on the cot in the front room. I don't."

Kate and Paddy exchanged glances again. "We'll need some sort of legal permission, I expect," Paddy said. "From the courts, or your grandmother."

"She'd give it. She hates me."

"Oh, Grace. She doesn't hate you," Kate said. "You—you remind her too much of your mother. Losing a child is the hardest thing in the world for a parent and it feels, I think, like a failure. A failure to protect the most precious thing in the world."

Grace sat silently.

"I've seen it more times than I'd like," Paddy said, "back in Ireland and in this country. It breaks a soul, it does. It's not the natural order of things. The older generation wants to pass on first. I can't blame her for being angry, only for taking it out on your father and letting it keep her from knowing you." He smiled at her. "Because you're a grand girl."

"Oh, Paddy." Grace slipped out of her chair and threw her arms around him.

"I'll talk to Daniel Gibson," Paddy said over her shoulder. "See what we need to do to make it legal, at least for now."

"And you and I will write to your grandmother again," Kate said, though what they would say, she had no idea.

But there was still the matter of who had killed Reverend Haugen. Kate spent much of the evening thinking about it, and much of the night, as she lay awake next to Paddy. The man could sleep through anything, a trait he attributed to growing up as the fourth of seven and then two weeks in steerage at twelve as he and his oldest brother crossed the stormy Atlantic.

By morning, she had worked out part of the puzzle. She worked out another piece while kneading bread dough. The tricky part would be to talk to Laura Peterman without terrifying her. Clearly, she was in a difficult situation and had confided in the reverend. Now that Kate had been in the Peterman home and seen how husband and wife treated each other, the obvious affection between them, and the health and happiness of their children, she no longer believed James Peterman a violent husband or father.

But the drawing nagged at her, as did her memory of the dismay on Laura's face when she saw Kate pondering the monogrammed coin purse.

They'd agreed that Laura would drive the buggy into town late morning to fetch Grace from the Mercantile. Kate and Paddy would drive out after closing to pick her up. Laura had promised Grace a chance to play the grand piano, a beautiful instrument that had struck a deep chord in Kate's soul.

Grace's letter to her grandmother lay on the table. Kate resisted the temptation to read it, instead slipping it into the envelope with a note saying simply that she and Mr. Murphy were pleased to keep the girl, who was excellent company and a good student, with a deft touch at the piano and with the needle, until plans could be finalized. What those plans might be, she did not elaborate. Could not say yet. Not until they'd gotten advice from more experienced minds.

When the baking was done, Kate wrapped up an extra loaf, tucked it in the basket Laura Peterman had given her alongside a jar of strawberry jam, and she and Grace set out.

"Where are we going?" Grace asked.

"To pay a call."

Anne Lang came to the door wearing a calico dress and an apron, her guarded expression easing at the sight of her visitors. Then her brow dipped. "I'm not sure I should invite you in."

"We're not afraid of Frank," Kate said firmly. "Or of talk. But we can't stay. I wanted to bring you some fresh bread and ask if there is any news." While she didn't want Grace to overhear idle gossip, she and Paddy had told her everything they knew about the search for her father's killer.

"None," Anne said. "Daniel's been able to keep the sheriff at bay, and I've been able to keep Frank busy. He's out back with his chickens right now. The way he clucks and flaps his arms like wings, they think he's one of them."

That put a smile on all their faces.

"It helps," Anne continued, "that Ivan believes Frank is innocent. But that doesn't explain the discovery in his woodpile."

"What if," Grace said, her voice tentative, "someone wanted us to blame Frank, or even Mr. Gregory, to distract attention from the real killer?"

The older women looked at her in astonishment.

"I read a book where that happened," she said.

"Not a book I gave you," Anne replied. "But I'll grant the possibility."

Who, though?

Kate and Grace said their goodbyes and continued on their way. Grace dashed across the street to slip the letter in the slot at the post office—always fun, even for a girl of eleven.

In the Mercantile, Kate set Grace to work dusting shelves. Not long after, Laura arrived, Elizabeth behind her.

"The younger two are home with their father," Laura said. Kate remembered James's comment to Paddy about leaving Jewel Bay. This family had the means to move, but would they? If the reason were compelling enough. Kate needed to probe carefully.

"This could be one of the last warm days," she said. "Maybe we could stroll down to the bridge. If my dear husband can spare me."

"Oh, go on with yeh, lass," Paddy called from behind the hardware counter, where he was weighing out nails.

The girls dashed ahead. "Grace seems no worse for the adventure," Laura said as they strolled down Front to Bridge Street. "Though she certainly made her feelings about returning to her grandmother's house clear. Have you decided what's to be done with her?"

How Grace's future had become Kate's decision, she wasn't sure. Merely because she'd found the reverend's body, or had fate had a hand in it?

"What would you do?" Kate asked. "Knowing what you know about the grandmother, and that there is no other family."

"I would keep her," Laura said, then held up a gloved hand. "And no, that's not an offer. I have my hands full with my three. But she seems genuinely happy with you and Paddy. And too much change at a time like this could be very difficult."

Anne Lang had said much the same thing.

They had reached the wooden bridge across the river, only a few years old, though there was already talk of replacing it with a new steel structure. In unspoken agreement, they stopped mid-span to watch the water coursing down the flume behind the power house, creating the invisible electricity that sparked so much growth and excitement.

The girls had crossed the bridge and were now down by the river, safely back from the water's edge.

"The power company, the bank—think of all that's happened here in such a short time," Kate said.

"And the Mercantile. We are lucky women, to have such forward-thinking husbands, who work hard and love us so, despite our faults."

"Laura." Kate faced her new friend, droplets of water splashing up from the river and misting the side of her face. "I can see you love James dearly, and your children, too. But—and forgive me the intrusion. We have not known each other long enough for me to speak so freely, and I wouldn't do it if it weren't for Grace."

Apprehension clouded Laura Peterman's lovely face.

"But," Kate went on, "I know you were speaking with Reverend Haugen regularly. Not about new altar cloths or cushions for the pews. About something deeply personal. And I wonder if it might in any way be connected to the tragedy that befell him."

It occurred to her in that moment that she might have chosen an unwise place for this conversation. Laura was several inches taller than Kate and a good deal stronger. If she had swung a silver candlestick at Reverend Haugen, what would stop her from pushing Kate over the side of the bridge and into the rushing river?

"Oh, Kate," Laura said. "I was so afraid that James had done something rash. But when the second candlestick surfaced, I knew I'd been mistaken. I thought—I feared that the reverend would feel compelled to reveal our secret and that James killed him to keep him quiet."

She paused, a hand to her chest, collecting herself.

"And he feared that's what you had done," Kate said, just loud enough to be heard above the river noise.

Laura's eyelids fluttered closed then opened again, her hand traveling from her chest to her mouth and back. "With James's prominence in the community, would any decent minister dare keep a secret like that? Even with children involved?"

What secret, Kate did not ask, but waited.

"James," Laura Peterman said, the single word rising and falling like the water from the flume as it struck the river, rose, and fell again, "is not my lawful husband."

Nothing this gracious, graceful woman could have said would have shocked Kate more. And yet, it explained the fear. And the monogram.

"I was married young, in Philadelphia, where I was reared. My late father's lawyer arranged the marriage, as I had no family but had come into a bit of money. He believed I needed a husband to manage it, even though the law allowed me to do so myself. The marriage was not a success. My husband was a gambler and the money was quickly gone. He drank to excess. He became violent at the drop of a hat."

Kate repressed a shudder. "And the law?"

"The law could not help me." Bitterness clung to Laura's words. "We no longer lived in the city. There are women in the cities who help women in need. I had no such recourse. But I did have a friend. She gave me shelter and bought me a railway ticket to Pittsburgh, where her family took me in."

"And that's where you met James."

"That's where I met James. My husband had made clear that divorce was out of the question. He would see me dead first, he vowed, and I believed him."

"That's why you and James came west, starting over as man and wife."

"Thirteen years ago. It's been everything a marriage ought to be. Then the children came, and James dotes on them. We have been so happy, and so intent on building our new life that I rarely gave the past any thought."

So what had caused the two of them to confide, separately, in their minister?

As if she heard Kate's musing, Laura answered the question. "Until my lawful husband tracked us down."

"The man in the drawing," Kate said, understanding now. "He threatened to reveal that you and James are not legally married and your children are illegitimate."

She could well believe it of the odious man Laura described. But she could not believe that Reverend Haugen would have revealed the truth. Nothing she had seen in his demeanor or heard since his death persuaded her that he would have acted so cruelly. He might have helped the distraught woman obtain a quiet divorce and remarry, if a few years late, but he bore his own scars from the past. He would have done nothing to put a family in danger.

"The truth would have ruined James's reputation. Everything he's worked for, all his business interests. The children would have been shamed. We would have had to leave Jewel Bay. Unless we paid him a monthly sum."

"Blackmail. That's vile."

"We were on the verge of agreeing to pay when he saw the candlesticks in the church. He became enraged. That's when he came to the house, when young James saw him from the tree. He no longer wanted money. He wanted blood."

Now Kate was confused. "The candlesticks?"

"They were a wedding gift," Laura explained. "From my father's lawyer, the scoundrel who arranged the marriage. No doubt bought with money siphoned from my inheritance. I had kept them all these years as my security, thinking I could sell them if I became truly desperate. But the church here was so plain, so unadorned, it needed a touch of beauty, and we were doing well. James was doing well—"

She was interrupted by a shout. Kate followed the sound and gasped. There was no mistaking the man in the drawing. The man she'd seen near Ivan Gregory's house. Thaddeus London. And he was standing amid the rocks at the water's edge, holding Elizabeth by one hand, Grace by the other.

"That's him, isn't it?"

Hands to her lips as if in prayer, Laura nodded. How foolish they had been, letting the girls go on ahead, caught up in their conversation, not noticing the man watching their every move. But what to do now? Even if they could get to the girls in time, they couldn't fight him off.

Think, Kate.

They needed to get help. But Laura would not budge. It was up to Kate. Suddenly the Mercantile seemed so far away.

A whizzing sound came from the bridge's wooden planks. Ivan Gregory's nephew, riding Reverend Haugen's bicycle. The boy grinned and raised a hand but Kate stepped into his path, forcing him to swerve to a stop. She grabbed the handlebars.

"Ride! Ride to the Mercantile as fast as you can. Tell Paddy there's trouble below the bridge and he must come. Hurry!"

The bicycle wobbled as the boy rode off, standing on the pedals to urge it forward. Would he be fast enough?

The scene on the riverbank had not changed, the girls tugging one way, London the other. He glanced up at Laura, the evil spreading across his face. And though she did not have the history Laura had with him, had never been his wife or his victim, Kate knew the terror Laura felt for Elizabeth, because she felt it herself for Grace. For both girls, of course, but Grace—Grace was *hers*.

"Stay here. Help is on the way. Distract him if you can, then send the men down when they come." And with that, Kate Flannery Murphy grabbed her skirt and ran as fast as she could, across the bridge and down the slope.

As she crept closer, she saw London look up at the bridge again. He threw a wicked laugh into the wind and dragged the girls closer to the water.

The cold, rushing water, the riverbed studded with hard, jagged rocks. If any of them went into the river, they'd be swept into its depths and smashed against the rocks. It was mid-October, the birches and vine maple changing color, the air warm enough that she hadn't even grabbed a shawl in her eagerness to talk with Laura Peterman. But the water was cold. It would batter and beat them and suck them out into the bay.

"I know who you are," she shouted. "I know why you're doing this."

"Do you?" Though the river was loud, his words were short and sharp.

"It doesn't have to be this way." She pushed closer. "Let them go. They're children. They've done nothing to you."

"They're nothing to me," he replied. "They are nothing."

They're everything to me.

"You don't have to do this." Could she get closer? Damn this heavy skirt. She put a hand on a rock and stepped around it, gasping as the cold water flooded into her boot.

The girls had seen her now and began to struggle, twisting London's arms this way and that. Grace's foot caught between two rocks and she fell. As London tried to regain his balance, he lost his grip on Elizabeth.

He swung his free arm, striking her in the face. Kate watched in horror as she fell, hitting a large rock, slippery with mud, and slid out of sight.

It was only a moment, a moment that took forever, a moment Kate would never forget.

"No!" she screamed and rushed forward. London was lashing at her now as she stretched her hand toward Elizabeth. She heard him cry out, a cry of pain, and then Grace was beside her in the water, fighting to grab hold of Elizabeth. Where was London? She couldn't see him. She had to get the girls out of the water, but she couldn't let that evil man get them first.

Where was he?

Then strong arms reached past her and grabbed Elizabeth. She could no longer see Grace. Other arms, arms she knew, pulled Kate out of the water, picked her up, and carried her to safety.

"Grace! Where's Grace?" Kate cried.

"She's safe, lass," the sweetest voice in the world answered. "She's safe. Yeh're all safe now. Thanks to you, my brave wife, yeh're all safe."

Later that day, Thaddeus London's body washed up on the lakeshore near the Indian encampment. Though Kate spared not one whit of grief for the man who had caused so much pain, she was deeply sorry that the Indians had to be the ones who found him. They had treated Grace well, and all the white men did, Kate thought, was rain down sorrow and sadness on them.

It turned out that Daniel Gibson had been in the Mercantile with more questions for her when the Gregory boy arrived, breathless. He and Paddy had rushed down Front on foot. They'd raced across the bridge, barely pausing to size up the situation below. It was obvious that London intended to drag both girls into the water and that Kate, determined as she was, could not stop him. She was too small, he too strong, the terrain too rough. But luck, or fate, or God, had intervened.

What Kate didn't understand was why Thaddeus London had killed Reverend Haugen. With both men gone, only Laura Culver London, the *LLC* of the monogrammed coin purse, could venture a plausible explanation.

"He understood what I'd been through," she'd said to the group that had gathered in the Mercantile after the girls were pulled from the river. Paddy had closed up shop for the day and stoked the woodstove to warm them. Kate had put on Paddy's old iron kettle—what he called his bachelor kettle—and they'd found enough cups for coffee and tea. The rough leaves Paddy sold the loggers weren't so bad after all, Kate decided, under the circumstances.

"He knew," Laura continued, "that women have few options when their husbands mistreat them, and he could not countenance that." James had arrived during the rescue and now he put a reassuring hand on his wife's shoulder. She laid hers on top of his. They were truly husband and wife, Kate thought, even if not before the law. "He could see that James and I cherished each other. It pained him that we were not legally married, but that troubled him less than the abuse I'd suffered and the threats Thaddeus was making. Nor could he tolerate blackmail, particularly when innocent children were involved."

"And," Paddy suggested, "when the fate of this community could well have been at stake. Including his own future and that of his daughter."

"When the reverend refused to promise silence, London struck him with the candlestick," Daniel Gibson said. He was leaning against the counter near the front door, his hands red with cold despite the hot mug in his hands. "Hid one behind the church and stashed the other in Ivan Gregory's woodpile. He was nursing a grudge against Ivan, too, for kicking him off the job at the power company."

"That must have been what he was doing when I saw him," Kate said. "After Buster and I found the first candlestick and I went to summon help. London was coming around the corner of the house. I wondered why he was there, but assumed he was working for Ivan. He headed back toward the church and I think if I hadn't been following him, he would have gone to the woodpile and retrieved the other candlestick, meaning to stash it somewhere else that would incriminate Ivan. But it was too late—I'd taken it. And I was watching him, so he changed course."

Paddy slid his arm around her and she leaned into his warmth, realizing for the first time how much danger she'd been in. It frightened her more now than it had then, when she'd been unaware, acting on instinct.

"I'll make sure word spreads quickly," Gibson said, "that Frank Lang had nothing to do with the murder or the theft. He's a good soul, despite the stammer and the bad leg, and it's not right that London sought to blame him for his own crimes. Mrs. Murphy, I owe you an apology. I underestimated you, and I promise not to do it again."

He'd smiled, and as she smiled back at him, an idea popped into her mind. But it could wait for a private moment with her husband. She'd gazed around the room, at the deputy, at the three Petermans, at young Grace and Paddy, her own true love. Paddy wanted the Mercantile—the Merc—to be the heart of Jewel Bay, and it was.

It was.

A week later, two letters arrived from Chicago, one for Kate and one for Grace. In the letter to Kate, Agnete Swensen apologized for the unkindness of her original letter and asked Kate's forgiveness. She was ill, she wrote, deathly ill, and did not expect to live out the year. It pained her to know that she was not likely to see her only grandchild again in this world and asked if Kate could perhaps send her a photograph or two.

I knew that Arval trusted me to come around and to love the child, the woman wrote, *and I would have, were I not ill.* The reverend, it seemed, had retained his faith in her, despite her behavior.

Mrs. Swensen had asked her lawyers to obtain references on Kate and Paddy, and instructed them that if all appeared in order, the Murphys should be given full legal custody of Grace, if they were willing. There would, she hinted, be a small legacy attached, though her lawyers would administer it. Kate thought briefly of the lawyer who had cheated Laura Peterman and forced her into an ugly marriage, but then remembered the kindhearted lawyer in Pondera whom she and Paddy had consulted about Grace, at James Peterman's suggestion. She decided she was willing to trust Mrs. Swensen's business judgment, even if her personal judgment had failed her.

Kate did not read the letter Mrs. Swensen's had written Grace, though it clearly touched the child deeply. Tucked inside were photographs of Freya through the years, and one of Freya with baby Grace, which Kate placed in a frame and set on the side table where Grace could see it every night from her cot.

The church in Jewel Bay was not expected to receive a new minister until spring, at the earliest, so the bishop made the trip to Pondera to preside over the lawful marriage of James and Laura. It was a quiet ceremony, except when Kate sniffed back tears, followed by coffee and cake at the Peterman home, where Kate finally set her hands on the grand piano.

Paddy readily agreed to Kate's suggestion that he hire Frank Lang to make deliveries and run errands at the Mercantile. Frank couldn't drive the Model T, but he could handle a wagon and the mule had instantly taken to him. Kate told Anne her suspicion that Daniel Gibson was sweet on her, but Anne replied he might have lost his chance to Ivan Gregory, and Kate considered that a good thing.

Grace and Elizabeth were becoming fast friends. While the girls chatted about books and lessons and classmates, Laura taught Kate a few embroidery skills. In the evenings, when Grace read to them, Kate worked on the monogrammed towels, no longer embarrassed by her stitches.

Paddy began to talk about adding a room onto the little log house in the spring. And when Kate wrote to her mother and Alice, Buster snoring on the floor between them, Grace wrote to her grandmother. Kate had ordered Grace her own stationery box and pen, and as the girl bent over the paper, Kate had to be careful not to let a tear of joy blot her own ink.

This, she knew, was where they all belonged.

Acknowledgments and Historical Note

Ten years ago, when *Death al Dente*, the first Food Lovers' Village Mystery, was published, I had no thoughts of adding a historical to the series. Jewel Bay, my fictional village, is closely modeled on Bigfork, Montana, my home for the last twenty-five years—although I have changed a few names and places so I could kill people. A few historical details about the unincorporated town, nestled between the shores of Flathead Lake and Glacier National Park in Northwest Montana, emerged as I wrote the five novels in the series.

Then, in 2017, a local trio created a documentary film called *Bigfork: A Montana Story*, a community history and fundraiser for the Bigfork Art and Cultural Center. My husband, Dr. Don Beans, wrote and performed the film score, including a piece that's become the town's unofficial theme song. The accompanying book, by Ed Gillenwater, Denny Kellogg, and Tabby Ivy, includes dozens of photos from the town's early days as a logging and commercial center, its growth, and its transition into an art town, a tourist destination, and a recreational haven. I pored over those photographs and others archived at the Art and Cultural Center. Both Ed and Denny helped me track down additional historical details, such as when electricity and telephone service were available. I am grateful to them, and to everyone involved in the History Project.

Though I've attempted to get the history right, this is fiction. Had I known I would write a historical, I might not have made up my own street names when I created Jewel Bay—Electric Avenue is the perfect name for the main street of a town literally powered by the river that runs through it! Although there were at least three mercantiles in various locations in the village, Murphy's Mercantile is none of them. Locals and visitors: if it existed, it would be next to the Garden Bar. Lone Pine Cemetery is real and as lovely an eternal resting place as you could hope for.

In 1910, a year I chose as the origin of the Murphy family in Jewel Bay long before I dreamed of this story, the Bigfork elementary school was located in the Methodist church, which was then south of the current tennis courts, leased while plans were made for a new school. For the novella, I added a church hall and turned it into a makeshift school. That and other historical fictions and inaccuracies are entirely my fault. The bell, by the way, was donated back to the school district a few years ago and still rings on special occasions.

It's been a joy to incorporate snippets of the history of this town I love so much into my fiction. Thanks to my agent, John Talbot, and to Bill Harris and his team at Beyond the Page Publishing for helping me bring it to life. Artist Dar Albert turned History Project photos into a beautiful cover that evokes the popular panoramic landscape paintings of the era.

Thanks most of all to the readers, especially the locals, who have embraced my books, particularly the Food Lovers' Village Mysteries.

Readers, it's a thrill to hear from you. Drop me a line at Leslie@LeslieBudewitz.com, connect with me on Facebook at LeslieBudewitzAuthor, or join my seasonal mailing list for books, news and more (sign up on my website, www.LeslieBudewitz.com). Reader reviews and recommendations are a big boost to authors; if you've enjoyed my books, please tell your friends, in person and online. A book is but marks on paper until you read these pages and make the story yours.

Thank you.

About the Author

Leslie Budewitz is passionate about food, great mysteries, and her native Montana, the setting for her national-bestselling Food Lovers' Village Mysteries. She also writes the Spice Shop Mysteries, set in Seattle's Pike Place Market. As Alicia Beckman, she's the author of stand-alone suspense set in Montana and the Northwest . She's the proud owner of three Agatha Awards, for Best Nonfiction (2011), Best First Novel (2013), and Best Short Story (2018), and has won or been nominated for Derringer, Anthony, and Macavity awards. Also a practicing lawyer, Leslie is a board member of Mystery Writers of America and is a past president of Sisters in Crime.

Leslie loves to cook, eat, hike, travel, garden, and paint—not necessarily in that order. She lives in northwest Montana with her husband, Don Beans, a doctor of natural medicine and musician, and their cat, an avid bird-watcher.

Visit her online at www.LeslieBudewitz.com, where you can find maps of the village and surrounding area, recipes, and more.

www.ingramcontent.com/pod-product-compliance
Lightning Source LLC
Chambersburg PA
CBHW021336060726
47591CB00006B/2041